MONSTER BLOOD III

Look for more Goosebumps books
by R.L. Stine:

Goosebumps

MONSTER BLOOD III

R.L. STINE

AN
APPLE
PAPERBACK

SCHOLASTIC INC.
New York Toronto London Auckland Sydney

A PARACHUTE PRESS BOOK

ISBN 0-590-48347-1

12 11 10 9 8 7 6 5 4 3   5 6 7 8 9/9 0/0

Printed in the U.S.A.   40

First Scholastic printing, March 1995

1

"The Monster Blood! It's growing again!" Evan Ross stared at the quivering green blob in his driveway. It looked like an enormous wad of sticky green bubble gum, and was bigger than a beach ball. Bigger than *two* beach balls!

The green blob trembled and shook as if it were breathing hard. It made disgusting sucking sounds. Then it started to bounce.

Evan took a step back. How did the sticky goo get out of its can? he wondered. Who left it in the driveway? Who opened the can?

Evan knew that once Monster Blood starts to grow, it can't be stopped. It will grow and grow, and suck up everything in its path.

Evan knew this from painful experience.

He had seen a giant glob of Monster Blood swallow kids whole. And he had seen what had happened when his dog, Trigger, had eaten Monster Blood. The cocker spaniel had grown and grown and grown — until he was big enough to pick up Evan in his teeth and bury him in the backyard!

A small chunk of Monster Blood had turned Cuddles, the tiny hamster in Evan's class, into a raging, growling monster. The giant hamster — bigger than a gorilla — had roared through the school, destroying everything in its path!

This gunk is dangerous, Evan thought. It may be the most dangerous green slimy stuff on Earth!

So how did it get in Evan's driveway?

And what was he going to do about it?

The Monster Blood bounced and hiccupped. It made more disgusting sucking sounds.

As it bounced, it picked up sticks and gravel from the driveway. They stuck to its side for a moment, before being sucked into the center of the giant wet ball.

Evan took another step back as the ball slowly started to roll. "Oh, noooo." A low moan escaped his throat. "Please. Noooo."

The Monster Blood rolled over the driveway toward Evan, picking up speed as it moved. Evan had tossed one of his Rollerblades by the side of the house. The green goo swallowed up the skate with a loud *thwocccccck*.

Evan gulped as he saw the skate disappear into the bouncing green ball. "I — I'm next!" he stammered out loud.

No way! he told himself. I'm getting out of here.

He turned to run — and went sprawling over the other skate.

"Ow!" he cried out as he fell hard on his elbows and knees. Pain shot up his arms. He had landed on both funny bones.

Shaking away the tingling, he scrambled to his knees. He turned in time to see the seething goo roll over him.

He opened his mouth to scream. But the scream was trapped inside him as the heavy green gunk splatted over his face.

He thrashed both arms wildly. Kicked his feet.

But the sticky goo wrapped around him. Pulling him. Pulling him in.

I — I can't breathe! he realized.

And, then, everything turned green.

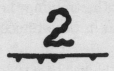

2

"Evan — stop daydreaming and eat your Jell-O," Mrs. Ross scolded.

Evan shook his head hard. The daydream had seemed so real. His mother's voice still sounded far away.

"Evan — hurry. Eat the Jell-O. You'll be late."

"Uh . . . Mom . . ." Evan said softly. "Could you do me a really big favor?"

"What favor?" his mother asked him patiently, pushing back her straight blond hair into a ponytail.

"Could we never have *green* Jell-O again? Could you just buy other colors? Not green?"

He stared at the shimmering, quivering green mound of Jell-O in the glass bowl in front of him on the kitchen counter.

"Evan, you're weird," Mrs. Ross replied, rolling her eyes. "Hurry up. Kermit is probably wondering where you are."

"Kermit is probably busy blowing up his house,"

Evan replied glumly. He pulled the spoon out of the Jell-O. It made a gross sucking sound.

"All the more reason for you to hurry over there," his mother said sharply. "You are responsible for him, Evan. You are in charge of your cousin until his mom gets home from work."

Evan shoved the green Jell-O away. "I can't eat this," he murmured. "It makes me think of Monster Blood."

Mrs. Ross made a disgusted face. "Don't mention that slimy stuff."

Evan climbed down from the stool. Mrs. Ross pushed a hand gently through his curly, carrot-colored hair. "It's nice of you to help out," she said softly. "Aunt Dee can't really afford a baby-sitter."

"Kermit doesn't need a baby-sitter. He needs a *keeper!*" Evan grumbled. "Or maybe a trainer. A guy with a whip and a chair. Like in the circus."

"Kermit looks up to you," Mrs. Ross insisted.

"Only because he's two feet tall!" Evan exclaimed. "I can't believe he's my cousin. He's such a nerd."

"Kermit isn't a nerd. Kermit is a genius!" Mrs. Ross declared. "He's only eight, and already he's a scientific genius."

"Some genius," Evan grumbled. "Mom, yesterday he melted my sneakers."

Mrs. Ross's pale blue eyes grew wide. "He *what?*"

"He made one of his concoctions. It was a bright yellow liquid. He said it would toughen up the sneakers so they would never wear out."

"And you let him pour the stuff on your sneakers?" Evan's mother demanded.

"I didn't have a choice," Evan replied unhappily. "I have to do everything Kermit wants. If I don't, he tells Aunt Dee I was mean to him."

Mrs. Ross shook her head. "I wondered why you came home barefoot yesterday."

"My sneakers are still stuck to Kermit's basement floor," Evan told her. "They melted right off my feet."

"Well, be careful over there, okay?"

"Yeah. Sure," Evan replied. He pulled his Atlanta Braves cap over his head, waved to his mother, and headed out the back door.

It was a warm spring day. Two black-and-yellow monarch butterflies fluttered over the flower garden. The bright new leaves on the trees shimmered in the sunlight.

Evan stopped at the bottom of the driveway and lowered the baseball cap to shield his eyes from the sun. He squinted down the street, hoping to see his friend Andy.

No sign of her.

Disappointed, he kicked a large pebble along the curb and started to make his way toward Kermit's house. Aunt Dee, Kermit's mom, paid Evan three dollars an hour to watch Kermit after school every afternoon. Three *hundred* dollars an hour would be a lot more fair! he thought angrily.

But Evan was glad to earn the money. He was saving for a new Walkman. Trigger had mistaken his old Walkman for a dog bone.

But Evan was earning every penny. Kermit was impossible. That was the only word for him. Impossible.

He didn't want to play video games. He didn't want to watch TV. He refused to go outside and play ball or toss a Frisbee around. He didn't even want to sneak down to the little grocery on the corner and load up on candy bars and potato chips.

All he wanted to do was stay downstairs in his dark, damp basement lab and mix beakers of chemicals together. "My experiments," he called them. "I have to do my experiments."

Maybe he *is* a genius, Evan thought bitterly. But that doesn't make him any fun. He's just *impossible*.

Evan definitely wasn't enjoying his after-school baby-sitting job watching Kermit. In fact, he had several daydreams in which Kermit tried one of his own mixtures and melted to the basement floor, just like Evan's sneakers.

Some afternoons, Andy came along, and that made the job a little easier. Andy thought Kermit was really weird, too. But at least when she was there, Evan had someone to talk to, someone who didn't want to talk about mixing aluminum pyrite with sodium chlorobenzadrate.

What is Kermit's problem, anyway? Evan wondered as he crossed the street and made his way through backyards toward Kermit's house. Why does he think *mixing* is so much fun? Why is he always mixing this with that and that with this?

I can't even mix chocolate milk!

Kermit's house came into view two yards down. It was a two-story white house with a sloping black roof.

Evan picked up his pace. He was about fifteen minutes late. He hoped that Kermit hadn't already gotten into some kind of trouble.

He had just pushed his way though the prickly, low hedges that fenced in Kermit's yard when a familiar gruff voice made him freeze.

"Evan — were you looking at my yard?"

"Huh?" Evan recognized the voice at once. It belonged to Kermit's next-door neighbor, a kid from Evan's school.

His name was Conan Barber. But the kids at school all called him Conan the Barbarian. That's because he had to be the biggest, meanest kid in Atlanta. Maybe in the universe.

Conan sat on top of the tall white fence that separated the yards. His cold blue eyes glared down at Evan. "Were you looking at my yard?" Conan demanded.

"No way!" Evan's voice came out in a squeak.

"You were looking at my yard. That's trespassing," Conan accused. He leaped down from the high fence. He was big and very athletic. His hobby was leaping over kids he had just pounded into the ground.

Conan wore a gray muscle shirt and baggy, faded jeans cutoffs. He also wore a very mean expression.

"Whoa. Wait a minute, Conan!" Evan protested. "I was looking at Kermit's yard. I *never* look at your yard. Never!"

Conan stepped up to Evan. He stuck out his chest and bumped Evan hard, so hard he stumbled backwards.

That was Conan's other hobby. Bumping kids with his chest. His chest didn't feel like a chest. It felt like a truck.

"Why *don't* you look at my yard?" Conan demanded. "Is there something wrong with my yard? Is my yard too ugly? Is that why you never look at it?"

Evan swallowed hard. It began to dawn on him that maybe Conan was itching for a fight.

Before he could answer Conan, he heard a scratchy voice reply for him. *"It's a free country, Conan!"*

"Oh, noooo," Evan groaned, shutting his eyes.

Evan's cousin, Kermit, stepped out from behind Evan. He was tiny and skinny. A very pale kid with a pile of white-blond hair, and round black eyes behind big red plastic-framed glasses. Evan always thought his cousin looked like a white mouse wearing glasses.

Kermit wore enormous red shorts that came down nearly to his ankles, and a red-and-black Braves T-shirt. The short sleeves hung down past the elbows of his skinny arms.

"What did you say?" Conan demanded, glaring down menacingly at Kermit.

"It's a free country!" Kermit repeated shrilly. "Evan can look at any yard he wants to!"

Conan let out an angry growl. As he lumbered forward to pound Evan's face into mashed potatoes, Evan turned to Kermit. "Thanks a lot," he told his cousin. "Thanks for all your help."

"Which way do you want your nose to slant?" Conan asked Evan. "To the right or to the left?"

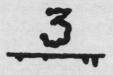

"Don't do it!" Kermit shrieked in his scratchy mouse voice.

Conan raised a huge fist. With his other hand, he grabbed the front of Evan's T-shirt. He glared down at Kermit. "Why not?" he growled.

"Because I have *this*!" Kermit declared.

"Huh?" Conan let go of Evan's shirt. He stared at the glass beaker Kermit had raised in both hands. The beaker was half-full with a dark blue liquid.

Conan let out a sigh and swept a beefy hand back through his wavy blond hair. His blue eyes narrowed at Kermit. "What's that? Your baby formula?"

"Ha-ha," Kermit replied sarcastically.

If Kermit doesn't shut up, we're *both* going to get pounded! Evan realized. What is the little creep trying to do?

He tugged at Kermit's sleeve, trying to pull him

away from Conan. But Kermit ignored him. He raised the beaker close to Conan's face.

"It's an Invisibility Mixture," Kermit said. "If I pour it on you, you'll disappear."

We should *both* disappear! Evan thought frantically. He let his eyes dart around the backyard. Maybe I can make it through that hedge before Conan grabs me, he thought. If I can get around the next house and down to the street, I might escape.

But would it be right to leave little Kermit at Conan's mercy?

Evan sighed. He couldn't abandon his cousin like that. Even though Kermit was definitely asking for it.

"You're going to make me invisible with that stuff?" Conan asked Kermit with a sneer.

Kermit nodded. "If I pour a few drops on you, you'll disappear. Really. I mixed it myself. It works. It's a mixture of Teflon dioxinate and magnesium parasulfidine."

"Yeah. Right," Conan muttered. He peered at the liquid in the beaker. "What makes it blue?"

"Food coloring," Kermit replied. Then he lowered his squeaky voice, trying to sound tough. "You'd better go home now, Conan. I don't want to have to use this stuff."

Oh, wow! Evan thought, pulling the bill of his Braves cap down over his face. I can't bear to

12

watch this. This is sad. Really sad. Kermit is such a jerk.

"Go ahead. Try it," Evan heard Conan say.

Evan raised the cap so he could see. "Uh . . . Kermit . . . maybe we should go in the house now," he whispered.

"Go ahead. Make me invisible," Conan challenged.

"You really want me to?" Kermit demanded.

"Yeah," Conan replied. "I want to be invisible. Go ahead, Kermit. Pour it on me. Make me disappear. I dare you."

Kermit raised the beaker over the gray muscle shirt that covered Conan's broad chest.

"Kermit — no!" Evan pleaded. "Don't! Please *don't*!"

Evan made a frantic grab for the beaker.

Too late.

Kermit turned the beaker over and let the thick blue liquid pour onto the front of Conan's shirt.

4

Out of the corner of his eye, Evan saw a monarch butterfly fluttering over the low hedges. *I wish I were a butterfly,* he thought. *I wish I could flap my wings and float away.*

As far away from here as I can get!

The blue liquid oozed down the front of Conan's muscle shirt. All three boys stared at it in silence.

"Well? I'm not disappearing," Conan murmured, narrowing his eyes suspiciously at Kermit.

Then his shirt started to shrink.

"Hey — !" Conan cried angrily. He struggled to pull off the shrinking shirt. It got tinier and tinier. "It — it's *choking* me!" Conan shrieked.

"Wow!" Kermit squeaked, his black eyes glowing excitedly behind his glasses. "This is cool!"

Evan gazed in amazement as the muscle shirt shrank down to a tiny shred of cloth. And then it vanished completely.

Now Conan stood in front of them bare-chested.

A heavy silence fell over the backyard. All three of them stared at Conan's broad, bare chest for a few moments.

Conan broke the silence. "That was my best muscle shirt," he told Evan through gritted teeth.

"Uh-oh," Evan uttered.

"I like your nose that way," Andy told Evan. "It kind of tilts in both directions at once."

"I think it will go back to the way it was," Evan replied, patting his nose tenderly. "At least it stopped hurting so much." He sighed. "All the other cuts and bruises will go away, too. In time."

It was two days later. Evan sat across from Andy in the lunchroom at school. He stared down sadly at the tuna fish sandwich his mom had packed for him. He hadn't taken a bite. His mouth wasn't working exactly right yet. It kept going sideways instead of up and down.

Andy wiped a chunk of egg salad off her cheek. She had short brown hair and big brown eyes that stared across the table at Evan.

Andy didn't dress like most of the other kids in their sixth-grade class. She liked bright colors. A lot of bright colors.

Today she wore a yellow vest over a magenta T-shirt and orange Day-Glo shorts.

When Andy moved to Atlanta in the beginning of the school year, some kids made fun of her colorful clothes. But they didn't anymore. Now everyone agreed that Andy had style. And a few kids were even copying her look.

"So what happened after Conan the Barbarian pounded your body into coleslaw?" Andy asked. She pulled a handful of potato chips from her bag and shoved them one by one into her mouth.

Evan took a few bites from a section of his tuna fish sandwich. It took him a long time to swallow. "Conan made me promise I'd never look in his yard again," he told Andy. "I had to raise my right hand and swear. Then he went home."

Evan sighed. He touched his sore nose again. "After Conan left, Kermit helped me hobble into his house," Evan continued. "A little while later, Aunt Dee got home."

"Then what happened?" Andy asked, crinkling up the empty potato chip bag.

"She saw that I was messed up," Evan replied. "So she asked what happened."

Evan shook his head and scowled. "And before I could say anything, that little rat Kermit piped up and said, 'Evan picked a fight with Conan.' "

"Oh, wow," Andy murmured.

"And Aunt Dee said, 'Well, Evan, if you're just going to get into fights instead of taking care of Kermit, I'm going to have to talk to your mom about you. Maybe you're not mature enough for this job.' "

"Oh, wow," Andy repeated.

"And the whole thing was Kermit's fault!" Evan shouted, pounding his fist so hard on the table that his milk carton tipped over. Milk spilled over the tabletop, onto the front of his jeans.

Evan was so upset, he didn't even move out of the way. "And do you know the worst thing?" Evan demanded. "The *worst* thing?"

"What?" Andy asked.

"Kermit did it deliberately. He knew what that blue mixture would do. He knew it would shrink Conan's shirt. Kermit wanted me to get pounded by Conan. He did the whole thing to get me in trouble with Conan."

"How do you know?" Andy asked.

"The smile," Evan told her.

"Huh? What smile?"

"The smile on Kermit's face. You know that twisted little smile he has where his two front teeth stick out? That's the smile he had when he helped me back to the house."

Andy tsk-tsked.

Evan finished the section of tuna fish sandwich. "Is that all you're going to say?" he snapped.

"What can I say?" Andy replied. "Your cousin, Kermit, is a weird little dude. I think you should teach him a lesson. Pay him back."

"Huh?" Evan gaped at her. "How do I do that?"

Andy shrugged. "I don't know. Maybe you could . . . uh . . ." Her dark eyes suddenly flashed with excitement. "I know! Doesn't he have

17

a snack after school every day? You could slip some Monster Blood into his food."

Evan gulped and jumped to his feet. "Hey — no way! No way, Andy!" he shouted.

Several kids turned to stare at Evan, startled by his loud cries.

"Don't even think it!" Evan shouted, ignoring the stares. "No Monster Blood. Ever! I never want to hear those words again!"

"Okay, okay!" Andy cried. She raised both hands, as if to shield herself from him.

"By the way," Evan said, a little calmer, "where is the Monster Blood? Where did you hide it? You didn't take any of it out — did you?"

"Well . . ." Andy replied, lowering her eyes. A devilish grin spread across her face. "I put a little bit of it in the tuna fish sandwich you just ate."

5

Evan let out a cry so loud, it made two kids fall off their chairs. Two other kids dropped their lunch trays.

His eyes bulged and his voice rose higher than the gym teacher's whistle. "You — you — you — !" he sputtered, grabbing his throat.

Andy laughed. She pointed at his chair. "Evan, sit down. I was only joking."

"Huh?"

"You heard me," Andy said. "It was a joke. The Monster Blood is home, safe and sound."

Evan let out a long sigh. He sank back into the chair. He didn't care that he was sitting in the milk he had spilled.

"Annndrea," he said unhappily, stretching out the word. "Annnndrea, that wasn't funny."

"Sure it was," Andy insisted. "And don't call me Andrea. You know I hate that name."

"Andrea. Andrea. Andrea," Evan repeated, paying her back for her mean joke. He narrowed his eyes at her sternly. "That new can of Monster Blood your parents sent you from Europe — it really is hidden away?"

Andy nodded. "On the top shelf of a closet in the basement. Way in the back," she told him. "The can is shut tight. No way the stuff can get out."

He stared hard at her, studying her face.

"Don't *look* at me like that!" she cried. She balled up the sandwich tinfoil and tossed it at him. "I'm telling the truth. The Monster Blood is totally hidden away. You don't have to worry about it."

Evan relaxed. He pulled the Fruit Roll-Up from his lunch bag and started to unwrap it. "You owe me now," he said softly.

"Excuse me?"

"You owe me for playing that stupid joke," Evan said.

"Oh, yeah? What do I have to do?" Andy demanded.

"Come with me after school. To Kermit's," Evan said.

Andy made a disgusted face.

"Please," Evan added.

"Okay," she said. "Kermit isn't that bad when I'm around."

Evan held up the sticky Fruit Roll-Up. "Want this? I *begged* my mom not to buy the green ones!"

*   *   *

After school, Evan and Andy walked together to Kermit's house. It was a gray day, threatening rain. The air felt heavy and wet, as humid as summer.

Evan led the way across the street. He started to cut through the backyards — but stopped. "Let's go the front way," he instructed. "Conan might be hanging out in back. Waiting for us."

"Don't say *us*," Andy muttered. She shifted her backpack to the other shoulder. She scratched her arm. "Ow. Look at this."

Evan lowered his eyes to the large red bump on Andy's right arm. "What is that? A mosquito bite?"

Andy scratched it some more. "I guess so. It itches like crazy."

"You're not supposed to scratch it," Evan told her.

"Thanks, Doc," she replied sarcastically. She scratched it even harder to annoy him.

A few sprinkles of rain came down as they made their way up Kermit's driveway. Evan opened the front door and stepped into the living room.

"Kermit — are you here?"

No reply.

A sour smell attacked Evan's nostrils. He pressed his fingers over his nose. "Yuck. Do you smell that?"

21

Andy nodded, her face twisted in disgust. "I think it's coming from the basement."

"For sure," Evan muttered. "Kermit must already be in his lab."

"Kermit? Hey — Kermit, what are you doing down there?" Evan called out.

Holding their noses, they made their way quickly down the stairs. The basement was divided into two rooms. To the right stood the laundry room and furnace; to the left the rec room with Kermit's lab set up along the back wall.

Evan hurried across the tiled floor into the lab. He spotted Kermit behind his lab table, several beakers of colored liquids in front of him. "Kermit — what's that disgusting smell?" he demanded.

As Evan and Andy ran up to the lab table, Kermit poured a yellow liquid into a green liquid. "Uh-oh!" he cried, staring down at the bubbling mixture.

Behind his glasses, his eyes grew wide with horror.

"Run!" Kermit screamed. "Hurry! Get out! It's going to BLOW!"

The liquid swirled and bubbled.

Kermit ducked under the lab table.

With a cry of horror, Evan spun round. Grabbed Andy's hand. Started to pull her to the stairs.

But he had only taken a step when he stumbled over Dogface, Kermit's huge sheepdog.

"Oof!" Evan felt the wind knocked out of him as he fell over the dog and landed facedown on the tile floor. He gasped. Struggled to choke in a mouthful of air.

The room tilted and swayed.

"It's going to BLOW!" Kermit's shrill warning rang in Evan's ears.

He finally managed to take a deep breath. Raised himself to one knee. Turned back to the lab table.

And saw Andy standing calmly in the center of the rec room, her hands at her waist.

"Andy — it's going to BLOW!" Evan choked out.

She rolled her eyes. "Evan, really," she muttered, shaking her head. "Did you really fall for that?"

"Huh?" Evan gazed past her to the long glass table.

Kermit had climbed back to his feet. He was leaning with both elbows on the table. And he had the grin on his face. *That* grin.

The twisted grin with the two front teeth sticking out. The grin Evan hated more than any grin in the world.

"Yeah, Evan," Kermit repeated, mimicking Andy, "did you really fall for that?" He burst into his squealing-high laugh that sounded like a pig stuck in a fence.

Evan pulled himself up, muttering under his breath. Dogface hiccupped. The dog's tongue tumbled out, and he began to pant loudly.

Evan turned to Andy. "I didn't really fall for it," he claimed. "I knew it was another one of Kermit's dumb jokes. I was just seeing if *you* believed it."

"For sure." Andy rolled her eyes again. She was doing a lot of eye-rolling this afternoon, Evan realized.

Evan and Andy stepped up to the table. It was littered with bottles and glass tubes, beakers and jars — all filled with colored liquids.

On the wall behind the table stood a high bookshelf. The shelves were also jammed with bottles and jars of liquids and chemicals. Kermit's mixtures.

"I was only a few minutes late getting here," Evan told Kermit. "From now on, don't do anything. Just wait for me." He sniffed the air. "What's that really gross smell?"

Kermit grinned back at him. "I didn't notice it until *you* came in!" he joked.

Evan didn't laugh. "Give me a break," he muttered.

Andy scratched her mosquito bite. "Yeah. No more jokes today, Kermit."

The big sheepdog hiccupped again.

"I'm mixing up something to cure Dogface's hiccups," Kermit announced.

"Oh, no!" Evan replied sharply. "No way! I can't let you give the dog one of your mixtures to drink."

"It's a very simple hiccup cure," Kermit said, pouring a blue liquid into a green liquid. "It's just maglesium harposyrate and ribotussal polythorbital. With a little sugar for sweetness."

"No way," Evan insisted. "You're not giving Dogface anything to drink but water. It's too dangerous."

Kermit ignored him and continued to mix chemicals from one glass beaker into another. He glanced up at Andy. "What's wrong with your arm?"

25

"It's a really big mosquito bite," Andy told him. "It itches like crazy."

"Let me see it," Kermit urged.

Andy eyed him suspiciously. "Why?"

Kermit grabbed Andy's hand and tugged her closer. "Let me see it," he insisted.

"It's just a mosquito bite," Andy said.

"I have some of that blue shrinking mixture left," Kermit announced. "The stuff I shrank Conan's shirt with."

"Don't remind me," Evan groaned.

"It'll shrink your mosquito bite," Kermit told Andy. He picked up the beaker.

"You're going to pour that stuff on my arm?" Andy cried. "I don't think so!"

She tried to step away.

But Kermit grabbed her arm. And poured.

The blue liquid spread over the mosquito bite.

"No! Oh, no!" Andy shrieked.

7

"My arm!" Andy shrieked. "What did you *do* to me?"

Evan lurched to the lab table, nearly stumbling over the dog again. He grabbed Andy's arm and examined it. "It — it —" he stammered.

"It's gone!" Andy cried. "The mosquito bite — it's gone!"

Evan stared at Andy's arm. Perfectly smooth, except for a few drips of the blue liquid.

"Kermit — you're a *genius!*" Andy cried. "That mixture of yours shrank the mosquito bite away!"

"Told you," Kermit replied, grinning happily.

"You can make a fortune!" Andy exclaimed. "Don't you realize what you've done? You've invented the greatest cure for mosquito bites ever!"

Kermit held up the beaker. He tilted it one way, then the other. "Not much left," he said softly.

"But you can mix up some more — right?" Andy demanded.

Kermit frowned. "I'm not sure," he said softly.

"I think I can mix up a new batch. But I'm not sure. I didn't write down what I put in it."

He scratched his white-blond hair and stared at the empty glass beaker, twitching his nose like a mouse, thinking hard.

Dogface let out another loud hiccup. The hiccup was followed by a howl. Evan saw that the poor dog was getting very unhappy about the hiccups. Dogface was a big dog — and so he had big hiccups that shook his sheepdog body like an earthquake.

"I'd better get to work on the hiccup cure," Kermit announced. He pulled some jars of chemicals off the shelf and started to open them.

"Whoa. Wait a minute," Evan told him. "I told you, Kermit — I can't let you feed anything to the dog. Aunt Dee will *kill* me if —"

"Oh, let him try!" Andy interrupted. She rubbed her smooth arm. "Kermit is a genius, Evan. You have to let a genius work."

Evan glared at her. "Whose side are you on?" he demanded in a loud whisper.

Andy didn't answer. She unzipped her orange-and-blue backpack and pulled out some papers. "I think I'll do my math homework while Kermit mixes up his hiccup cure."

Kermit's eyes lit up excitedly behind his glasses. "Math? Do you have math problems?"

Andy nodded. "It's a take-home equations exam. Very hard."

Kermit set down the test tubes and beakers. He hurried out from behind the lab table. "Can I do the problems for you, Andy?" he asked eagerly. "You know I love to do math problems."

Andy flashed Evan a quick wink. Evan frowned back at her. He shook his head.

So *that's* why Andy is being so nice to Kermit! Evan told himself. It was all a trick. A trick to get Kermit to do the math test for her.

Kermit could never resist math problems. His parents had to buy him stacks and stacks of math workbooks. He could spend an entire afternoon doing all the problems in the workbooks — *for fun!*

Dogface hiccupped.

Kermit grabbed the math test from Andy's hand. "Please let me do the equations," he begged. "Pretty please?"

"Well . . . okay," Andy agreed. She flashed Evan another wink.

Evan scowled back at her. Andy is going to get in trouble for this, he thought. Andy is a *terrible* math student. It's her worst subject. Mrs. McGrady is going to get very suspicious when Andy gets every problem right.

But Evan didn't say anything. What was the point?

Kermit was already scribbling answers on the page, solving the equations as fast as he could read them. His eyes were dancing wildly. He was breathing hard. And he had a happy grin on his face.

"All done," he announced.

Wow, he's fast! Evan thought. He finished that math test in the time it would take me to write my name at the top of the page!

Kermit handed the pencil and math pages back to Andy. "Thanks a lot," she said. "I really need a good grade in math this term."

"Cheater," Evan whispered in her ear.

"I just did it for Kermit," Andy whispered back. "He loves doing math problems. So why shouldn't I give him a break?"

"Cheater," Evan repeated.

Dogface hiccupped. Then he let out a pained howl.

Kermit returned to his lab table. He poured a yellow liquid into a red liquid. It started to smoke. Then it turned bright orange.

Andy tucked the math test into her backpack.

Kermit poured the orange liquid into a large glass beaker. He picked up a tiny bottle, turned it upside down, and emptied silvery crystals into the beaker.

Evan stepped up beside Kermit. "You can't feed that to Dogface," Evan insisted. "I really mean it. I won't let you give it to him."

Kermit ignored him. He stirred the mixture until it turned white. Then he added another powder that made it turn orange again.

"You have to listen to me, Kermit," Evan said. "I'm in charge, right?"

Kermit continued to ignore him.

Dogface hiccupped. His white furry body quivered and shook.

"Let Kermit work," Andy told Evan. "He's a genius."

"Maybe he's a genius," Evan replied. "But I'm in charge. Until Kermit's mom gets home, I'm the boss."

Kermit poured the mixture into a red dog dish.

"I'm the boss," said Evan. "And the boss says no."

Kermit lowered the dog dish to the floor.

"The boss says you can't feed that to Dogface," Evan said.

"Here, boy! Here, boy!" Kermit called.

"No way!" Evan cried. "No way the dog is drinking that!"

Evan made a dive for the bowl. He planned to grab it away.

But he dove too hard — and went sliding under the lab table.

Dogface lowered his head to the dog dish and began lapping up the orange mixture.

Evan spun around and stared eagerly at the dog. All three of them were waiting . . . waiting . . . waiting to see what would happen.

Dogface licked the bowl clean. Then he stared up at Kermit, as if to say, "Thank you."

Kermit petted the big dog's head. He smoothed the white, curly fur from in front of Dogface's eyes. The fur fell right back in place. Dogface licked Kermit's hand.

"See? The hiccups are gone," Kermit declared to Evan.

Evan stared at the dog. He waited a few seconds more. "You're right," he confessed. "The hiccups are gone."

"It was a simple mixture," Kermit bragged. "Just a little tetrahydropodol with some hydradroxilate crystals and an ounce of megahydracyl oxyneuroplat. Any child could do it."

"What a genius!" Andy exclaimed.

Evan started to say something. But Dogface interrupted with a sharp yip.

Then, without warning, the big sheepdog sprang forward. With another shrill yip, Dogface raised his enormous front paws — and leaped on to Kermit.

Kermit let out a startled cry and stumbled back against the wall. Bottles and jars shook on the shelves behind him.

Dogface began barking wildly, uttering shrill, excited yips. The dog jumped again, as if trying to leap into Kermit's arms.

"Down, boy! Down!" Kermit squealed.

The dog jumped again.

The shelves shook. Kermit sank to the floor.

"Down, boy! Down!" Kermit shrieked, covering his head with both arms. "Stop it, Dogface! Stop jumping!"

The excited dog used his head to push Kermit's arm away. Then he began licking Kermit's face frantically. Then he began nipping at his T-shirt.

"Stop! Yuck! Stop!" Kermit struggled to get away. But the big dog had Kermit pinned to the floor.

"What's going on?" Andy cried. "What's gotten into that dog?"

"Kermit's mixture!" Evan replied. He dove at the dog, grabbed Dogface with both hands, and tried to tug him off Kermit.

Dogface spun around. With another high-pitched yip, he bounded away, running at full speed across the basement.

"Stop him!" Kermit cried. "He's out of control! He'll break something!"

CRAAAASH.

A shelf of canning jars toppled to the floor.

Barking loudly, the dog bounded away from the shelf and began running in wide circles, his big paws clomping on the tile floor. Round and round, as if chasing his tail.

"Dogface — whoa!' Evan called, chasing after the sheepdog. He turned back to Andy. "Help me! We've got to stop him! He's acting crazy!"

Dogface disappeared into the laundry room. "Dogface — come back here!" Evan called.

He burst into the laundry room in time to see the dog crash into the ironing board. It toppled over, along with a stack of clothes that had been resting on it. The iron clattered over the hard floor.

Dogface yelped and climbed out from under the spilled clothes. Spotting Evan, the dog's stubby tail began wagging — and he leaped across the room.

"No!" Evan screeched as the huge dog knocked him over backwards to the ground. Dogface frantically licked Evan's face.

Behind him, Evan heard Andy laugh. "Too much energy! He's acting like a crazy puppy!" she declared.

"He's too big to think he's a puppy!" Evan wailed.

Dogface was sniffing furiously under the washing machine. He pounced on a large black ant.

Then he turned and came bounding over to Andy and Evan.

"Look out!" Evan cried.

But the big sheepdog lumbered past them, back into the other room. They followed him, watching him roll over a few times, kicking his big, furry paws in the air.

Then Dogface jumped to his feet — and came charging at Kermit.

"Whoa! Whoa, boy!" Kermit cried. He turned to Andy. "You're right. This is just the way Dogface acted when he was a puppy. The mixture gave him too much energy!"

The sheepdog crashed into an old couch against the wall. He climbed up onto the couch, sniffing the cushions, exploring. His stubby tail wagged furiously.

"Dogface, you're not a puppy!" Evan cried. "Please listen to me! You're too big to be a puppy! Dogface — please!"

"Look out!" Andy shrieked.

The dog jumped off the couch and went running full speed toward Kermit.

"No! Stop!" Kermit cried. He dove behind the lab table.

The dog tried to slow down. But his big legs were carrying him too fast.

Dogface crashed into the lab table. Bottles and beakers flew into the air, then crashed to the floor. The table toppled over on top of Kermit.

The shelves fell off the wall, and all of the jars and tubes and beakers tumbled to the floor, shattering, clattering, chemicals pouring out over the floor.

"What a mess!" Evan cried. "What a horrible mess!"

He turned — and let out a loud gasp.

Aunt Dee stood in the doorway. Her mouth was opened wide in surprise, and her eyes nearly bulged out of her head.

"What on Earth is going on down here?" she shrieked.

"Uh . . . well . . ." Evan started.

How could he begin to explain? And if he did find a way to explain, would Aunt Dee believe him?

Aunt Dee pressed her hands against her waist and tapped one foot on the floor. "What has happened here?" she demanded angrily.

"Uh . . . well . . ." Evan repeated.

Kermit spoke up first. He pointed an accusing finger at Evan. "Evan was teasing the dog!" he cried.

9

Kermit's mom glared angrily at Evan. "I'm paying you to take care of Kermit," she said sternly. "Not to play silly jokes on the dog and wreck my house."

"But — but — but —" Evan sputtered.

"Evan didn't do it!" Andy protested.

But her words were drowned out by Kermit, who let out a loud, phony wail — and burst into tears. "I tried to stop Evan!" Kermit sobbed. "I didn't want him to tease Dogface! But he wouldn't stop!"

Kermit rushed into his mother's arms. "It's okay," Aunt Dee said soothingly. "It's okay, Kermit. I'll make sure Evan never does it again."

She narrowed her eyes angrily at Evan as Kermit continued to sob, holding on to his mother like a baby.

Evan rolled his eyes at Andy. Andy replied with a shrug.

"Evan, you and Andy can start cleaning up this mess," Mrs. Majors ordered. "Kermit is a very sensitive boy. When you play jokes like this, it upsets him terribly."

Kermit sobbed even louder. His mom tenderly patted his head. "It's okay, Kermit. It's okay. Evan won't ever tease Dogface again," she whispered.

"But — but —" Evan sputtered.

How could Kermit put on such an act?

How could he deliberately get Evan into trouble? This mess wasn't Evan's fault. It was Kermit's!

"I really don't think —" Andy started.

But Aunt Dee raised a hand to silence her. "Just get this mess cleaned up — okay?"

She turned to Evan. "I'm not going to tell your mom about this, Evan," she said, still patting Kermit's head.

"Thanks," Evan muttered.

"I'm going to give you one more chance," she continued. "You don't really deserve it. If you weren't my nephew, I'd make you pay for all the damage. And I'd get someone else to take care of Kermit."

"Evan is mean," Kermit murmured, removing his glasses and wiping tears off his cheeks. "Evan is really mean."

What a little rat! Evan thought. But he remained silent, his eyes lowered to the floor.

"Kermit, let's get you cleaned up," Aunt Dee

said, leading him to the stairs. "Then we'll have to give the dog a bath."

She turned back to Evan and pointed a finger at him. "One more chance," she warned. "One more chance."

In the corner, Dogface let out a loud hiccup.

"See how you've upset the dog?" Kermit's mom called to Evan. "You've given poor Dogface the hiccups!"

"But — but —" Evan sputtered again.

As Evan struggled to find words to defend himself, Kermit and his mom disappeared up the stairs.

Two hours later, Andy and Evan wearily headed for home.

"What a mess," Evan moaned. "Look at me. I'm covered in chemicals."

"Two hours," Andy muttered. "Two hours to clean up the basement. And Dogface stood there watching us, hiccupping the whole time."

"Kermit is such a little creep," Evan said, kicking a stone across the sidewalk.

Andy shook her head bitterly. "Do you have any more cousins like him?"

"No," Evan replied. "Kermit is one of a kind."

"He's such a little liar," Andy said.

"Hey — you stuck up for him," Evan accused. "You said he was a genius, remember? You were so happy that he did your math problems for you, you thought he was wonderful."

Andy shifted her backpack onto her other shoulder. A smile crossed her face. "I forgot all about the math problems," she said. "Kermit may be a little creep — but he's also a genius. I'm going to get an A in math!" She let out a happy cheer.

"Winners never cheat, and cheaters never win," Evan muttered.

Andy gave him a playful shove. "Did you just make that up? It's very catchy."

"Give me a break," Evan growled. He turned and made his way up his driveway without saying good-bye.

Andy called him two nights later. "Your cousin Kermit is a total creep!" She shouted so loudly, Evan had to hold his phone away from his ear.

"Do you know what he did? Do you know what he did?" Andy shrieked.

"No. What?" Evan asked softly.

"He did all the math equations wrong," Andy cried.

"Excuse me?" Evan wasn't sure he heard correctly. "The genius got everything wrong?"

"On purpose!" Andy declared. "He got them wrong on purpose. He made up answers for all of them! He didn't even read the problems. He just wrote down stupid answers."

"But why?" Evan demanded.

"Why? Why? Because he's Kermit!" Andy screamed.

Evan swallowed hard. Poor Andy, he thought. Now she will fail in math.

"What a mean, rotten trick!" Andy shrieked into the phone. "Mrs. McGrady called me up to her desk and asked me to explain my answers. She asked me how I could possibly be so totally off on every single equation."

Andy sighed bitterly. "Of course I couldn't answer her. I just stood there with my mouth open. I think I drooled on her desk!"

"After we left his house, Kermit probably laughed his head off," Evan said.

"That brat has such a sick sense of humor," Andy wailed. "We have to pay him back, Evan. We really have to."

"Yeah. We do," Evan agreed.

"We have to get out the Monster Blood," Andy urged. "We have to use the Monster Blood to pay him back."

"Yeah. We do," Evan agreed.

10

Evan called Andy back later that night. "I changed my mind," he said. "I don't want to use the Monster Blood."

"What's your problem?" Andy demanded. "Kermit deserves it. You know he does."

"Monster Blood is too dangerous," Evan told her. "It turned Cuddles the hamster into a giant, roaring monster. I don't want to turn Kermit into a giant, roaring monster."

"Neither do I!" Andy exclaimed. "I don't want to *feed* it to him, Evan. I just want to slip a tiny bit into one of his mixtures. He thinks he's so smart and can do anything. I want to see Kermit's face when his mixture goes berserk!"

She laughed gleefully.

What an evil laugh, Evan thought.

"It'll be awesome!" Andy exclaimed.

"Forget about it," Evan insisted. "I have nightmares about Monster Blood almost every night.

I don't want to see that stuff again, Andy. I really don't. Leave it locked up — please!"

"But you *said* we could to it!" Andy pleaded.

"I made a mistake," Evan told her. "Don't take it out of the closet, Andy. Leave it safe and sound in its can — okay?"

Andy didn't reply.

"Okay?" Evan demanded. "Okay?"

"Okay," Andy finally agreed.

"We're going to play outside today, Kermit," Evan said firmly. "It's a beautiful day, and we're going to go out and not stay in the stupid basement. Get it?"

It was a sunny, warm Thursday afternoon. Golden sunlight filtered down through the dust-covered basement windows up near the ceiling.

Standing behind his lab table, arranging his jars and bottles of chemicals, Kermit muttered something to himself.

"No argument," Andy added. "We're going outside even if Evan and I have to drag you out."

"But I have a mixture I want to try," Kermit whined.

"You need some sunshine," Evan told him. "Look how pale you are. You look just like a white mouse."

Kermit was wearing a huge olive-colored T-shirt over baggy brown shorts. With his white-blond hair, beady eyes, and buck teeth, he looked more like a rat in human clothes.

He frowned, hurt by Evan's description.

"Okay. I'll go outside with you," he murmured unhappily.

"Yaay!" Andy whooped. It was the first time Kermit had ever agreed to leave his basement lab.

"But first I have to have a drink," Kermit said. He stepped out from behind the lab table and made his way toward the basement stairs. "You want an orange soda?"

"Yeah. Sure," Evan replied. He and Andy followed Kermit up the stairs to the kitchen.

"I can't believe he agreed to go out and play," Andy whispered. "Do you think he's sick or something?"

"Maybe he feels bad about the mean tricks he's pulled," Evan whispered.

The kitchen phone rang. Evan answered it. It was the wrong number.

He hung up the phone. He and Andy stepped up to the counter. Andy was wearing pink jeans, a yellow sleeveless T-shirt, and bright orange high-tops.

Kermit had already poured out three glasses of orange soda. The soda was the same color as Andy's high-tops, Evan noticed. They all drank the soda down quickly.

"I was really thirsty," Kermit said. Evan didn't pay any attention to the strange smile on Kermit's face. After all, Kermit *always* had a strange smile on his face.

"This orange soda is very sweet," Andy commented. She made a face. "Too sweet! It makes my teeth itch!"

Kermit laughed. "I think it's good," he said.

They set their glasses down in the sink and stepped out the back door. Evan found a red Frisbee on the back stoop. He flipped it to Andy.

Andy trotted across the backyard and flipped it back to Evan. "Let's play keep-away from Kermit!" she cried.

"Hey — no way!" Kermit protested. "Toss it to me!"

Andy sent the Frisbee flying over Kermit's head to Evan. Kermit made a wild grab for it, but it sailed out of his reach. It hit Evan's hands, but Evan dropped it.

Andy started to laugh.

"What's so funny?" Evan demanded.

Andy shrugged. "I don't know." She let out another giggle.

Evan flipped the Frisbee to Kermit. It bounced off Kermit's chest.

This kid is a real klutz, Evan thought. It's because he never plays sports. He never comes up out of his basement.

Andy uttered a high-pitched laugh.

Evan started to laugh, too.

Kermit picked up the Frisbee. He tried to toss

it to Andy, but the Frisbee sailed way over her head. It hit the side of the garage and bounced off.

Evan and Andy both laughed harder.

Evan trotted over to the garage. He sent a sidearm toss toward Andy. She missed, and the Frisbee flew into the low hedges at the side of the yard.

Andy didn't chase after it. She was laughing too hard.

Evan laughed even harder. Tears ran down his cheeks.

What's happening to me? he wondered, suddenly feeling frightened.

Why can't I stop laughing? What's going on?

Kermit grinned at both of them. *That* grin!

Evan laughed even harder. So hard, his stomach hurt.

Something is wrong, Evan realized. Something is terribly wrong.

"K-Kermit — why are we l-laughing?" he stammered.

Andy wiped tears from her eyes. She held her sides and laughed some more.

"Why are we laughing?" Evan demanded.

"I gave you my laughing mixture," Kermit told them. "I put it in the orange soda."

Evan tossed back his head and laughed. Andy giggled so hard, she choked. But she kept on laughing.

This isn't funny. This is scary, Evan thought. But he let out a shrill giggle.

"How — how long are we going to laugh like this, Kermit?" Evan managed to ask.

"Probably forever," Kermit replied, flashing his famous toothy grin.

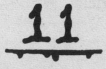

Evan took a deep breath and tried to hold it. But the laughter burst out of him so hard, his chest ached.

Laughing giddily, Andy made a grab for Kermit.

Kermit ducked out of her reach and went scampering toward the fence at the back of the yard.

Evan shook his head hard, trying to shake off the effect of the laughter potion. But it didn't help. He laughed until tears rolled down his face.

Andy chased after Kermit, laughing shrilly.

Evan followed, gasping for breath. I can't breathe, he realized. I'm laughing so hard, I can't breathe.

"K-Kermit —!" Evan choked out. "You've got to s-stop it!" A high giggle burst out of his throat. "You've g-got to!"

"I don't know how," Kermit replied calmly.

Andy and Evan laughed in reply.

"It's awesome — isn't it!" Kermit declared happily. "The mixture works perfectly!"

Andy made a grab for Kermit's throat.

Again, Kermit ducked away.

Andy and Evan laughed a little harder.

Andy picked up the Frisbee and tried to heave it at Kermit. But she was laughing too hard to control it. The Frisbee sailed over the fence.

"Hey — get that back. That's mine!" Kermit demanded.

Evan and Andy laughed.

A familiar face popped up on the other side of the fence.

"Conan!" Kermit cried.

Conan peered first at Andy, then at Evan. "Are you looking at my yard?" he asked Evan.

Evan struggled to hold it in. But he let out a high, shrill laugh.

"Didn't I warn you last week about looking at my yard?" Conan demanded.

Evan laughed.

"Conan, give me back my Frisbee," Kermit whined.

Conan leaped over the fence. Evan saw that he had the Frisbee in his left hand. Conan quickly hid the Frisbee behind his back.

Andy and Evan laughed. Andy wiped tears from her eyes. Her whole body shook with laughter.

"Give me back my Frisbee," Kermit insisted.

Conan ignored him. "What's so funny?" he asked Andy and Evan. He balled his right hand into a fist.

Andy giggled.

If we keep laughing, he'll pound us! Evan realized. But he couldn't help himself. He let out a loud belly laugh.

"Hey — I want my Frisbee!" Kermit whined.

"I don't have your Frisbee," Conan lied, keeping his left hand behind his back.

Evan tossed his head back and laughed.

"Yes, you do. It's behind your back," Kermit said. "Give it back, Conan."

"Who's going to make me?" Conan demanded in a low, menacing voice.

Evan let out a high giggle. Andy laughed, too.

"They are!" Kermit replied to Conan. "They're going to make you!" He turned to Evan. "Make Conan give back my Frisbee."

Evan laughed in reply.

"What's so funny?" Conan asked again.

Andy shook her head. "Nothing. Nothing's funny," she choked. Then she burst out laughing.

"I don't like people laughing at me," Conan said.

This is horrible! Evan thought. One more laugh — and Conan could explode!

Evan let out a long hyena laugh.

"I really go ballistic when people laugh at me," Conan warned.

Evan and Andy laughed some more.

50

"I have to *hurt* people who laugh at me," Conan threatened.

Evan and Andy laughed in reply.

Conan turned to Kermit. "Why are they laughing like that?"

Kermit shrugged. "Beats me. I guess they think you're funny."

"Oh, is that right?" Conan shouted angrily, turning back to Evan and Andy. "You two think I'm *funny*?"

Evan and Andy held their sides and laughed.

"Give me my Frisbee!" Kermit shouted.

"Okay. Go chase it." Conan flung the Frisbee across the hedges. It sailed over two yards and disappeared in a clump of evergreen shrubs.

Kermit went running after it.

Conan scowled at Evan and Andy. "I'm going to count to three," he growled. "And if you don't stop laughing by the count of three, I'll *make* you stop!" He raised both fists to show them *how* he would make them stop.

"One . . ." Conan said.

Evan laughed. Andy pressed her hand over mouth, but couldn't stop a giggle from escaping.

"Two . . ." Conan counted, his face twisted in anger.

I've *got* to stop laughing! Evan told himself. I'm in serious trouble here. Serious.

He opened his mouth, and a booming "Hahahahaha!" burst out.

Andy had *both* hands pressed over her mouth. But it didn't stop the snickers and guffaws from pouring out her nose.

Kermit came jogging back into the backyard. "I can't find the Frisbee," he complained. "Somebody has to help me. I can't find it anywhere."

Conan turned to him. "You *sure* you don't know why they're laughing like that?" he asked.

Kermit shook his head. "They told me they think you're funny-looking," he told Conan. "I guess that's why they're laughing."

I don't believe this! Evan thought, so angry he wanted to explode. That little creep! How can he do this to us?

Conan turned back to Andy and Evan. "Last chance to stop," he said. He took a deep breath, stretching out his big, powerful chest. "Three!"

Andy laughed.

Evan laughed even harder.

"I warned you," Conan growled.

12

Andy phoned Evan that night to see how he was feeling. Evan had to hold the phone away from his ear. His head hurt too much to press a phone against it.

"I guess I'll survive," Evan groaned. "I'm getting used to looking in the mirror and seeing a pile of coleslaw where my head used to be."

Andy sighed. "Your cousin is such a creep," she said.

"How are *you* feeling?" Evan asked. "How long did it take you to climb down from the tree?"

"Not too many hours," Andy replied weakly.

Conan had said he never hit girls. So he picked Andy up and stuck her onto a high tree branch.

"At least Conan stopped us from laughing," Evan said. "My stomach still hurts from laughing so hard."

"Mine, too," Andy told him. "I'm never going to laugh again. Never. If someone tells me the funniest joke in the world, I'll just smile and say, 'Very funny.' "

"I can't believe Kermit did that to us," Evan moaned.

"I believe it," Andy replied dryly. "Kermit will do anything to get us into trouble. That's what he lives for — getting us into major trouble."

"Did you hear that little mouse laughing while Conan pounded me into the ground?" Evan asked.

"I was up in the tree, remember? I could *see* him laughing!" Andy declared.

There was a long silence at the other end. And then Andy spoke in a hushed voice, just above a whisper, "Evan — are you ready to use the Monster Blood on Kermit?"

"Yeah," Evan replied without having to think about it even for a second. "I'm ready."

13

After school the next afternoon, Evan and Andy found Kermit behind his lab table as usual. "Hi, Kermit," Evan called, tossing his backpack down and stepping up to the table.

Kermit didn't glance up. He was busy stirring ingredients in a large mixing bowl, using a large wooden spoon.

Evan peered into the bowl. It looked like pie dough in there. It was thick and gooey and yellowish.

Kermit hummed to himself as he stirred.

Andy was wearing a sleeveless, hot pink T-shirt over bright yellow shorts and matching yellow sneakers. She stepped up beside Evan and peeked into the bowl. "Making a pie?" she asked.

Kermit ignored her, too. He kept stirring and humming, stirring and humming.

Finally he stopped and glanced up at Evan. "I told my mom you lost my Frisbee," he said, sneering. "She says you have to get me a new one."

"Huh? Me?" Evan cried.

Andy walked around to Kermit's side of the table. She lowered her head to the bowl. "Smells lemony," she said. "What is it, Kermit? Is it some kind of dough?"

"It was your fault my Frisbee got lost," Kermit told Evan, ignoring Andy's questions. "Mom says you're a very bad baby-sitter."

Evan let out an angry cry. He balled his hands into fists. He struggled to keep himself from strangling Kermit.

It was a real struggle.

"Mom wanted to know who drank up all the orange soda," Kermit continued. "I told her you and Andy drank it."

"Kermit!" Evan shrieked. "You played a horrible trick on us yesterday! You put chemicals in our orange soda! You made us laugh and laugh and laugh — until it hurt. Then you got us in major trouble with Conan! Did you tell your mom that? Did you? *Did you?*"

Kermit put his hands over his ears. "Don't shout, Evan," he whined. "You know I have very sensitive ears."

Another angry growl escaped Evan's throat. He felt about to explode with rage.

"I told my mom that you shout at me all the time," Kermit continued. "Mom says you're just immature. She thinks you're very babyish. She

56

only lets you stay with me because you're my cousin."

Kermit picked up the wooden spoon and started to stir the doughy mixture again.

Evan spun away, trying to control his anger.

I'm glad Andy and I are going to do what we're going to do, he thought. I'm glad we're going to give Kermit a little scare. He's been asking for it. He really has. And now he's going to get it.

Evan walked over to his backpack. He unzipped it and pulled out a candy bar. "Mmmm. A Choc-O-Lik Bar," he murmured. He crossed back to the lab table, unwrapping the candy bar as he walked.

Standing in front of Kermit, Evan took a big bite of the chocolate bar. It made a loud *crunch* as his teeth sank into it. "Mmmmmm!" he proclaimed. "Choc-O-Lik Bars are cool."

The candy bar was part of the plot.

Evan knew that the Choc-O-Lik Bar was Kermit's favorite.

The candy bar was supposed to distract Kermit. While Kermit stared at the candy and pleaded with Evan to give him a bite, Andy would slip a tiny chunk of Monster Blood into Kermit's mixture.

Evan crunched the candy bar loudly, making lip-smacking sounds as he chewed.

Kermit glanced up. He stopped stirring the yellowish dough. "Is that really a Choc-O-Lik Bar?" he asked.

Evan nodded. "Yeah. Sure is."

"My favorite," Kermit said.

"I know," Evan replied. He took another crunchy bite.

Kermit stared at the candy bar.

Andy stood beside Kermit. Evan saw the blue container of Monster Blood in her hand. Just *seeing* the can made Evan shiver.

So many bad memories. So many nightmares.

The green gunk inside the can was so dangerous.

"Can I have a piece of the Choc-O-Lik Bar?" Kermit asked Evan.

Andy lifted off the top of the Monster Blood container.

"Maybe. Maybe not," Evan told Kermit.

Andy stuck two fingers in the container. She pulled out a gooey green hunk of Monster Blood.

"Please? Pretty please?" Kermit begged Evan.

Andy dropped the chunk of Monster Blood into Kermit's big bowl of dough. Then she quietly snapped the cap back on the container and slid it back into her bag.

Evan took another bite of the candy bar.

"You shouldn't eat a candy bar unless you have enough to share with everyone," Kermit scolded.

"You haven't been very nice to me," Evan told him. "So I'm not going to share."

Kermit started stirring the dough again. He stared angrily at Evan as he stirred. He didn't see the green Monster Blood being stirred up in the yellow dough.

Evan took another bite of the Choc-O-Lik Bar. Only a few bites left.

"I'm going to tell Mom you were mean to me," Kermit threatened. "I'm going to tell her you wouldn't share."

Evan shook his head. "See what I mean? You're not nice to me, Kermit. If you were nice to me, I'd share *all* my candy bars with you."

Andy winked at Evan. Then she peered into the bowl.

Kermit stirred and stirred.

Andy's expression became tense. She gripped the edge of the table with both hands. Evan saw her nibble her bottom lip.

Watching Kermit stir the Monster Blood, Evan suddenly had a heavy feeling in his stomach.

We've done it, he thought.

We've opened another can of Monster Blood.

He stared at the yellow dough in the bowl. It made a soft plopping sound as Kermit pushed the wooden spoon through it.

Now what? Evan wondered.

Now what's going to happen?

14

Kermit stirred the yellow dough. The big wooden spoon scraped the bowl. The doughy mixture plopped softly, tumbling and swirling as Kermit worked.

Andy kept nibbling her lower lip, her eyes locked on the bowl. Her brown hair fell over her face. But she made no move to push it back.

Evan watched from the other side of the table. His heart began doing flip-flops in his chest. He took another bite of the chocolate bar.

He chewed as quietly as possible. He didn't want to disturb Kermit. As he chewed, he stared at the bowl.

He and Andy were waiting. Waiting to see what the little hunk of Monster Blood would do to Kermit's mixture.

Waiting to see the look of horror on Kermit's face.

Waiting to pay him back for being such a little monster.

Kermit didn't seem to notice how quiet it had become in the basement. Dogface came lumbering in, panting loudly, his paws thudding on the tile floor.

No one turned to look at him.

The dog hiccupped, turned, and padded out of the room.

Evan bit off another chunk of the candy bar.

Kermit stirred, humming to himself. The spoon scraped the side of the bowl. The dough slapped against the edge.

And spilled over.

Kermit stopped stirring. "Weird," he muttered.

Evan's heart did a flip-flop up to his throat. "What's weird?" he asked.

"It grew," Kermit replied, scratching his white-blond hair. "Look."

Kermit pointed to the yellow dough with the wooden spoon. It plopped up over the top of the bowl.

"It — it's growing really fast!" Kermit declared.

Evan took a few steps closer. Andy leaned down to get a better look.

The dough rose up, shimmering and quivering.

"Wow!" Kermit cried. "It wasn't supposed to do this! It was supposed to turn sticky and black!"

Andy winked at Evan. Her brown eyes lit up excitedly. A smile spread across her face.

The yellow blob quivered up over the top of the bowl, as big as a beach ball.

How big was it going to get?

"Oh, wow! This is awesome!" Kermit declared.

The dough shimmered higher. Wider.

It rose up high over the bowl. It overflowed the sides.

Bigger. Bigger. It started to look like an enormous hot air balloon.

"It's taller than me!" Kermit declared. His voice had changed. He didn't sound excited now. He was beginning to sound frightened.

"We'd better stop it, I think," he murmured.

"How?" Andy asked. She stepped out from behind the lab table and joined Evan on the other side.

Andy grinned at Evan. She was enjoying the expression of fear on Kermit's face. Evan had to admit he enjoyed it, too.

The ball of yellow dough shimmered and shook, growing bigger every second. It bubbled up faster and faster, pressing Kermit back against the basement wall.

"Hey — help!" he sputtered.

Andy's grin grew wider. "He's terrified now," she whispered to Evan.

Evan nodded. He knew he was supposed to enjoy this. It was supposed to be sweet revenge.

But Evan was terrified, too.

How much bigger would the huge yellow blob

grow? Could they stop it? Or would it grow and grow and grow until it filled the entire basement?

"Evan — help me!" Kermit cried. "I'm trapped back here!"

The dough began to shake harder. It bobbed up against the basement ceiling.

Evan glanced down and realized he was still holding a chunk of candy bar in his hand. The chocolate had started to melt.

Evan started to pop the candy into his mouth — just as the giant dough ball exploded with a deafening roar.

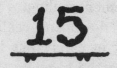

15

"ULP!"

Evan swallowed hard as the doughy goop exploded. The force of the blast sent the candy chunk flying down his throat.

He started to cough and choke.

With a hard *splat*, globs of sticky dough hit him in the face. The yellow goo spread over his hair and covered his eyes.

"Hey!" Evan choked out. He frantically wiped the dough from his eyes, blinking hard.

He could taste it on his tongue. "Yuck!" He spit it out and rubbed the sticky stuff off his lips. Then he pulled thick wads of goo off his face.

"It's stuck to my hair!" Andy wailed.

"Help me! Help me!" Kermit's cries sounded as if they were coming from far away. Evan quickly saw why. Kermit was buried under a big heap of yellow goop.

Pulling dough from his hair, Evan hurried behind the lab table. He reached down with both hands and tugged Kermit up from under the dough.

"Wow. I'm kind of dizzy!" Kermit cried. He leaned heavily against the lab table. His hands slid in the yellow goo that covered the table.

"I'll never get it out of my hair!" Andy wailed, tugging at her hair with both hands. "Never!" She turned to Evan. "It wasn't supposed to explode. Just get big. I guess something in the dough made it blow up."

Wiping dough off the front of his T-shirt, Evan gazed around the basement. The yellow dough had splattered over everything. Now it dripped down the walls, making soft plopping sounds as it hit the floor.

"That was an awesome explosion!" Kermit declared. His eyeglasses were covered with yellow goop. He pulled them off and squinted around the room.

He turned to Andy. "Did you put something in the bowl?"

"Never mind," Andy replied, still pulling sticky yellow globs from her hair.

Kermit tugged her arm. "What was it? What did you put in my mixture?"

"Why do you want to know?" Andy demanded.

"So we can do that again!" Kermit declared gleefully. "It was so *awesome*!"

"No way we're doing it again!" Evan moaned.

Their revenge on Kermit hadn't exactly worked

out, Evan realized bitterly. Kermit should be in tears by now. Or he should be quivering in fear and terror.

Instead, his eyes were dancing with excitement and he was grinning from ear to ear.

We were total jerks! Evan thought sadly. Kermit is *loving* this!

Kermit pulled out a cloth and cleaned his glasses. "What a mess!" he declared, gazing around the room. "Evan, you're going to be in major trouble when Mom gets home."

Evan swallowed hard. He had forgotten about Kermit's mom.

She had given him one last chance to prove that he was a good baby-sitter.

Now she was going to come home to a basement splattered with sticky yellow goop from floor to ceiling. And Kermit was sure to tell her the whole thing was Evan's fault.

Aunt Dee will tell everyone in the world why she had to take the job away from me, Evan thought unhappily. And I'll never get another baby-sitting job as long as I live.

Bye-bye, Walkman, he thought grimly. No way he'd ever earn the money for one now.

"This is *your* fault!" he snapped at Andy, pointing an accusing finger at her. A spot of yellow dough stuck to his fingernail.

"*My* fault?" Andy shrieked. "*You're* the one who wanted to teach Kermit a lesson!"

"But *you're* the one who wanted to use the Monster Blood!" Evan cried.

"Look at my hair!" Andy wailed. "It's solid goop! It looks like I'm wearing a helmet! It's ruined! Ruined!" She uttered an angry growl.

Kermit giggled. He bent down and picked up a chunk of the sticky yellow dough. "Think fast!' he shouted — and heaved it at Evan.

The dough ball hit the front of Evan's T-shirt and stuck there. "Stop it, Kermit!" he shouted angrily.

"Let's have a dough fight!" Kermit suggested, grinning. He scooped up another handful of the stuff.

"No! No way! Stop it!" Evan cried. He pulled the dough ball off his T-shirt. "This is dangerous! We've got to clean this up!"

Kermit flung another big chunk of yellow goo at Evan.

Evan tried to dodge out of the way. But his sneakers slipped on a big, slimy puddle of goop, and he hit the floor hard. He landed on his side with a loud "OOF!"

Kermit let out a gleeful laugh. "That was awesome!" he declared. "What a shot!"

Andy hurried over and helped tug Evan to his feet. "Maybe we can vacuum it all up," she suggested. She turned to Kermit. "Where does your mom keep the vacuum cleaner?"

Kermit shrugged. "Beats me."

Evan leaned against the lab table. His hand rested in a puddle of dough, but he didn't care.

He suddenly felt strange.

His entire body started to tingle. His stomach felt queasy. He shut his eyes, trying to force the strange feeling away.

But the tingling grew stronger.

He heard a shrill whistling sound in his ears. His muscles started to ache. He could feel the blood throbbing at his temples.

"Maybe we can mop it up," Evan heard Andy say. But her voice sounded tiny and far away.

He turned to see her pick up a mop and bucket from against the basement wall.

That bucket is too tiny, Evan thought. Why does Andy want to use such a tiny mop?

The room tilted — to the right, then to the left.

Evan blinked hard, trying to straighten everything out.

His whole body buzzed, as if an electrical current were shooting through him. He shut his eyes and pressed both hands against his throbbing temples.

"Evan — aren't you going to help me?" Andy's voice sounded so faint, so far away. "Evan —?" he heard her call. "Evan —?"

When he opened his eyes, he saw that Andy and Kermit were staring up at him. Their expressions had changed. Their eyes bulged in fright and surprise. Their mouths were wide open.

"What's going on?" Evan demanded. His voice boomed through the basement, echoing off the concrete walls.

Andy and Kermit stared up at him. The tiny mop fell out of Andy's hand and clattered to the floor.

Such a tiny mop, Evan thought again, staring down at it. Such a tiny bucket.

And then he realized that Andy and Kermit were tiny, too.

"Oh!" A cry of surprise escaped Evan's throat.

Everyone is so small. Everything is so tiny.

It took Evan a long time to figure out what had happened.

But when it finally dawned on him, he let out a shriek of horror.

"Oh, no! No!" he moaned. "I'm *growing*! I'm growing bigger and bigger!"

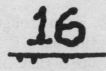

16

Evan lowered his eyes to the floor. It seemed so far below.

"My — my legs —" he stammered.

Andy and Kermit still hadn't said a word. They stared up at him, their faces twisted in surprise.

Evan swallowed hard. "What's going on?" he cried. His voice boomed through the small room. "I must be eight feet tall!"

"You — you're a *giant*!" Kermit declared. He stepped forward and grabbed on to Evan's knee. "Me, too! Okay? Okay, Evan? Make me a giant, too!" he begged.

"Give me a break," Evan muttered. He picked up Kermit easily and set him down on top of the lab table.

Then Evan turned to Andy. "What am I going to do? This is terrible!"

"Not so loud!" Andy pleaded, covering her ears with her hands. "Please, Evan — try to whisper or something, okay?"

"What am I going to do?" Evan repeated, ignoring her plea.

Andy forced a smile. "Try out for basketball, I guess."

Evan balled his huge hands into huge fists. "I'm not in the mood for your sick sense of humor, Andy," he snapped.

His body started to tingle again. His muscles ached.

I'm growing even bigger, he realized.

Evan's throat suddenly felt very dry. He realized his knees were shaking. They made a loud banging sound as they hit together.

Don't panic! he instructed himself.

The first rule is — don't panic.

But why *shouldn't* he panic? His head was nearly pushing up against the basement ceiling.

Kermit stood up on top of the lab table. His white high-tops were splattered with yellow dough. They looked like little doll shoes to Evan.

"Make me a giant, too!" Kermit pleaded. "Why can't I be a giant?"

Evan stared down at his cousin. Kermit really *did* look like a little white mouse now.

Evan's body tingled harder. The room tilted and swayed again. "This is *your* fault, Andy!" he shouted.

Andy shrank back against the wall. "Huh? My fault?"

"You and your Monster Blood!" Evan thundered. "I — I swallowed some!"

Andy stared up at him. "How?"

"When Kermit's mixture exploded," Evan replied. "I was putting the candy bar in my mouth. The dough exploded. I started to choke. The dough hit me in the face. I remember I tasted it. It was on my lips. And — and —"

"And it had Monster Blood in it!" Andy finished his sentence for him. Her face filled with horror. "Oh, Evan. I'm sorry. I really am."

But then her face brightened. "The Monster Blood splashed on your clothes, too. That was lucky. They're growing with you."

Evan let out an exasperated sigh. "Lucky?" he cried. "You call this lucky? What if I keep growing and never stop?"

Kermit remained standing on the lab table. He stared up at Evan. "You mean if I eat some of the dough, I'll turn into a giant, too?" He bent down and scooped up a handful of dough.

"Don't you *dare*!" Evan screamed. He leaned over and flicked the dough out of Kermit's hand with two fingers. Then he hovered over Kermit, glaring at him menacingly. "I can squash you, Kermit. I really can," Evan warned.

"Okay, okay," Kermit muttered, his voice trembling. He slid off the table and stepped behind Andy.

Wow, Evan thought, I actually have Kermit

72

afraid of me! That's a first. Maybe growing so big isn't all bad!

His body tingled and vibrated. The whistling in his ears grew louder. He could feel himself grow some more.

He turned to see Dogface pad into the room. The big sheepdog looked like a tiny poodle.

The dog hiccupped. It sniffed at a yellow puddle of dough on the floor.

"No!" Evan cried. "Don't eat that! Dogface — no!"

He bent over and picked up the sheepdog.

Seeing a giant human lift him up easily off the floor, Dogface let out a yelp of terror. All four legs thrashed the air as the frightened dog struggled to break free.

But Evan cradled the sheepdog in one arm and held on to him tightly.

When he realized he couldn't escape from the giant, the dog's terrified yelps turned to quiet whimpers.

"Take Dogface out of here. Lock him outside," Evan ordered Kermit. He lowered the whimpering dog to the floor.

Kermit obediently led the dog away. Halfway to the stairs, he turned back to Evan. "Hey, you cured Dogface's hiccups!"

I guess I scared them out of him! Evan told himself.

Kermit led Dogface up the stairs. Evan turned

73

to Andy. "I *told* you to leave the Monster Blood in the closet!" he cried. "Now look at me!"

He had to duck his head. Otherwise it would brush against the ceiling.

"Who told you to *eat* the stuff?" Andy replied. "Why did you have to be eating that candy bar?"

"It was part of the plan — remember?" Evan snapped angrily. He uttered a bitter sigh. "Great plan we had!"

"I guess it didn't work out too well," Andy admitted.

"I guess it didn't," Evan muttered. "Now what will happen to me? What will Mom and Dad say?"

"What will you eat?" Andy added. "You'll probably have to eat sixteen meals a day! And where will you sleep? And how can you go to school? There aren't any desks big enough for you. And what will you wear? They'll have to make your T-shirts out of bedsheets!"

"You're not cheering me up," Evan murmured glumly.

He felt his body tingle. Again, he could feel his skin stretching, feel all of his muscles throb.

"Ow!" he cried out as the top of his head banged against the ceiling.

He had to lean over to rub his head.

"Evan — you're growing!" Andy exclaimed.

"I know. I know," Evan grumbled. The basement ceiling was at least nine feet high. Evan had to stoop to keep from banging the ceiling. That meant he was more than nine feet tall.

A shiver of fear shook his body. He glanced around the basement. "I have to get out of here!" he cried.

Kermit returned to the room. He stopped and gawked at Evan. "You grew even more!" he cried. "I'll bet you weigh three hundred pounds!"

"I don't have time to weigh myself," Evan replied, rolling his eyes. "I have to get out of here. I'm so big, I can't stand up. I'm so big, I —"

He stopped. He felt himself grow a little more.

"I'm too big now!" he cried. "I'm trapped down here! There's no way I can get out!"

17

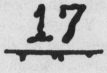

"Stay calm," Andy called up to him.

"Calm? How can I stay calm?" Evan shrieked. "I'm going to spend the rest of my life in this basement! I'm too big for the stairs!"

"Mom won't like that," Kermit said, shaking his head.

"Try the stairs!" Andy cried. "Maybe you can squeeze up if you hurry!"

Evan turned to the basement stairs. "I — I don't think I'll fit," he stammered. The stairway appeared very narrow. And Evan was now very wide.

"Come on," Andy urged. "We'll help you."

"You push and I'll pull," Kermit said, running to the stairs.

Evan lumbered toward the stairs. His sneakers thudded heavily on the tile floor. He stooped his shoulders to keep his head from crashing against the ceiling.

"Try not to grow any bigger!" Andy called, following closely behind him.

"Great advice!" Evan replied sarcastically. "Do you have any more advice like that?"

"Don't be nasty," Andy scolded. "I'm only trying to help you."

"You've already helped me more than enough," Evan grumbled.

He felt his body start to tingle. His muscles started to throb.

"No! Please — no!" He uttered a silent plea. I don't want to grow any more!

He sucked in a deep breath and held it. He shut his eyes tight and tried to concentrate — concentrate on not growing.

"I think I just saw you grow another few inches," Andy called to him. "You'd better hurry, Evan."

"How big is Evan going to get?" Kermit asked. He had climbed halfway up the stairs. "Is he going to get bigger than an elephant?"

"That's not helpful, Kermit," Evan muttered unhappily. "Please stop asking questions like that — okay?"

"If you get as big as an elephant, will you give me a ride?" Kermit demanded.

Evan glared angrily at his cousin. "Do you know what elephants do to mice?" he bellowed. Evan raised one foot and brought it down with a crunching *thud* to demonstrate to Kermit what elephants do to mice.

Kermit swallowed hard and didn't say anything more.

Evan walked over to the stairway. He glanced up the stairs. "I don't think I can make it," he told Andy. "I'm too big."

"Give it a try," she urged. "You've *got* to, Evan."

Evan stepped on to the first step. Leaning low, he raised himself to the next step.

"You're doing it!" Kermit cried happily. He stayed at the top of the stairs, watching Evan's progress eagerly.

Evan took another step. The wooden stairs creaked under his weight. He tried to lean on the banister. But it snapped beneath his hand.

He climbed two more steps.

He was a third of the way up when he became stuck.

His body was just too wide for the narrow stairway.

Kermit pulled both of Evan's hands. Andy pushed him from behind.

But they couldn't budge him.

"I — I can't move," Evan stammered. He felt panic choke his throat. "I'm jammed tight in here. There's no way I'll ever get out!"

Then he felt his body start to tingle. And he knew he was growing even more.

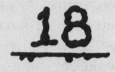

18

As Evan grew, he heard a cracking sound.

Soft at first. Then louder. Very close by.

He cried out as the wall to his left crumbled. His expanding body had broken the wall away.

As the wall cracked and fell, Evan took a deep breath and lurched up the stairs.

"Made it!" he cried as he squeezed through the doorway.

A few seconds later, he burst out through the kitchen door, into the sunlit backyard.

Dogface lay stretched out near the fence. The dog jumped to his feet as the gigantic Evan appeared. Frightened, Dogface gave a loud bark, his stubby tail wagging furiously, then turned and bolted from the yard.

Kermit and Andy followed Evan into the backyard, cheering and shouting, "You made it! You're free!"

Evan turned to face them. "But now what?" he

asked. "Now what do I do? I'm nearly as tall as the garage. How tall am I going to grow?"

Kermit stepped closer to Evan. "Look — I'm standing in your shade!" he declared.

Evan's shadow fell across the yard like the shadow of a tree trunk. "Kermit, give me a break," Evan muttered. "I have a little bit of a problem here, you know?"

"Maybe we should get you to a doctor," Andy suggested.

"A doctor?" Evan cried. "What could a doctor do for me?"

"Put you on a diet?" Andy joked.

Evan leaned over her, squinting down at her menacingly. "Andy, I'm warning you. One more bad joke, and —"

"Okay, okay." Andy raised her hands as if trying to shield herself from him. "Sorry. Just trying to keep it light."

"Evan isn't light. He's heavy!" Kermit chimed in. His idea of a joke.

Evan let out an unhappy growl. "I don't think a doctor can help me. I mean, I couldn't fit into a doctor's office."

"But maybe if we brought the can of Monster Blood along, the doctor could figure out an antidote," Andy suggested. "Some kind of cure."

Evan started to reply. But shrill voices on the other side of the tall wooden fence at the back of the yard made him stop.

"Cut it out, Conan!" a girl pleaded.

"Yeah. Leave us alone, Conan!" Evan heard a boy shout.

Evan lumbered over to the fence and peered into Conan's yard. He saw Conan Barber furiously swinging a baseball bat, swinging it hard, forcing a little boy and girl to back up against the fence.

"Let us go!" the little girl screamed. "Why are you so mean?"

Conan swung the bat, bringing it close to the boy and girl, making them cry out.

Evan leaned over the fence. His broad shadow fell over Conan. "Want to play ball with me, Conan?" Evan thundered.

The two little kids spun around. They stared up at the enormous Evan. It took them a long time to realize they were staring at a real, giant human.

Then they began to scream.

Conan's mouth dropped open and a strangled gurgling sound escaped his throat.

"Hey, Conan, how about a little batting practice?" Evan asked, his voice booming over the backyard. Evan reached over the fence and plucked the bat from Conan's hand.

The little boy and girl ran away screaming. They darted through the hedge at the side of Conan's yard and kept running until they vanished from view.

Evan took the bat and snapped it in two between his hands. It cracked apart like a toothpick.

Conan froze in place, staring up at Evan in disbelief. He pointed a trembling finger. "Evan — you — you — you —" he stammered.

Evan tossed the two pieces of the cracked bat at Conan's feet, forcing Conan to hop out of the way.

"You ate Monster Blood!" Conan accused. "That sticky green stuff. The stuff that Cuddles the hamster ate last year! You ate some — didn't you!"

Evan didn't want to be reminded of Cuddles the hamster. The little creature had turned into a huge, vicious beast after eating Monster Blood. Cuddles had returned to hamster size only because the Monster Blood was old and stale.

But the Monster Blood Evan had swallowed was new and fresh.

Now *I'm* a huge, vicious beast, Evan thought sadly.

"Are you crazy? Are you totally messed up? Why did you eat Monster Blood?" Conan demanded.

"It was an accident," Evan told him.

Conan continued to stare up at Evan, but his fearful expression faded. Conan suddenly started to laugh. "I'm glad it happened to you and not me!" he exclaimed.

"Huh? Why?" Evan demanded.

"Because I'm afraid of heights!" Conan replied. He laughed again. "I always thought you were a nerd, Evan!" Conan declared. "But now you're a BIG nerd!"

Evan let out an angry growl and lurched forward. He tried to climb over the fence. But he didn't step high enough. Conan's fence splintered beneath Evan's heavy sneaker.

"Hey —!" Conan cried in alarm.

He tried to turn and run, but Evan was too fast for him.

Evan grabbed Conan under the shoulders and lifted him off the ground as if he weighed nothing.

"Let go! Let go of me!" Conan screamed. He kicked his arms and legs like a baby.

"I never knew you were afraid of heights," Evan said. Holding Conan in both hands, he raised him high in the air.

"Let me go! Let me go!" Conan cried. "What are you going to do?"

"Let's see if you know how to fly!" Evan exclaimed.

"Noooooo!" Conan's shrill cry rose up over the yard. He kicked and thrashed as Evan raised him even higher. "Put me down! Put me down!"

"Okay," Evan agreed. "I'll put you down." He set Conan down on a high tree branch.

Conan clung to the trunk for dear life, trembling and crying. "Evan — don't leave me up here! Please! I told you, I'm afraid of heights! Evan — come back! Evan!"

A huge grin on his huge face, Evan turned away

from Conan. "That was a lot of fun!" he called down to his friends.

Conan continued to weep and wail up in the tree. Evan took a few steps toward the front yard. "That was excellent!" Evan said, still grinning. "Excellent!"

"Where are you going?" he heard Andy call up to him.

"Yeah! What are you going to do now?" Kermit asked eagerly.

"This is kind of cool!" Evan declared. Having his revenge on Conan had put him in a better mood. "Let's go see if we can have some more fun!"

"Yaaaay!" Kermit cried, racing to keep up with Evan.

Evan ducked his head to keep from banging it on a low tree branch. He took several big steps toward the street.

"Oh!" He stopped and cried out when he felt himself step on something. He heard a cracking, then a crunch beneath his enormous sneaker.

He turned to see Kermit raise both hands to his face. "Oh, no!" Kermit shrieked. "You squashed Andy! Evan — you squashed Andy!"

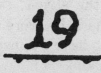

19

Evan gasped and jerked up his foot.

Kermit let out a high-pitched laugh. "Gotcha, Evan!"

Andy came running over from the driveway. "That wasn't funny!" she scolded Kermit. "That was a really dumb joke, Kermit. You scared Evan to death."

"I know!" Kermit laughed, very pleased with himself.

Evan let out a sigh of relief. He bent down to see what he had stepped on. Conan's skateboard. It lay crushed and splintered, flat on the grass.

He turned angrily to Kermit. "No more stupid jokes," he thundered. "Or I'll put you up in the tree with Conan."

"Okay. Okay," Kermit mumbled. "You think you're tough just because you're so big."

Evan held up a pointer finger. "Careful, Kermit," he warned. "I could knock you over with one finger."

"Conan is still yelling for help back there," Andy reported.

Evan smiled. "Let's see who's hanging out at the playground. Maybe we can surprise some other kids."

Evan crossed the street, taking long, heavy strides. He felt as if he were walking on stilts. This is kind of cool, he told himself. I'm the biggest person in the world!

He passed by the neighbors' basketball hoop, which stood on a pole at the curb. Hey — I'm at least six feet taller than the basket! he realized.

"Hey — wait up!" Andy called breathlessly. "Don't walk so fast!"

"I can't help it!" Evan called back.

A small blue car rolled by, then squealed to a stop. Evan could see a woman and two kids in the car. They were all staring out at him.

A little girl on a bike turned the corner. She started pedaling toward Evan. He saw the look of surprise on her face when she spotted him.

She braked her bike hard, nearly toppling over the handlebars. Then she wheeled around and sped out of sight.

Evan laughed.

Another car screeched to a halt.

As he started to cross another street, Evan turned to see who was in the car. He didn't watch where he was going.

A loud *crunch* made him stop.

With a gasp, he peered down — and saw that he had stepped on a car.

"Oh, no!" Evan cried. His sneaker had crushed in the top of the car — as if it were made of tinfoil.

Evan backed away in horror. Was someone inside?

He dropped to his knees to stare in the window. "Thank goodness!" he cried when he saw that the car was empty.

"Wow!" Kermit exclaimed, walking around and around the smashed-in car. "You must weigh at least a ton, Evan!"

Andy stepped up beside Evan, who remained on his knees. "Be careful," she warned. "You've got to watch every step."

Evan nodded in agreement. "At least I think I've stopped growing," he called down to her.

As they reached the playground, Evan saw several kids shouting and pointing excitedly at a tall maple tree on the corner.

What's going on? Evan wondered.

As he lumbered closer, he saw the problem. Their yellow kite had become stuck up in the tree.

"Hey — no problem!" Evan boomed.

The kids screamed and cried out in surprise as Evan stepped up to them. They all backed away, their faces tight with fear.

Evan reached up easily and tugged the kite loose from the tree limb. Then he leaned down and gently handed it to the nearest kid.

"Hey, thanks!" A grin spread across the kid's freckled face.

The other kids all cheered. Evan took a bow.

Andy laughed. "You need a red cape and a pair of blue tights," she shouted up to him. "It's Super Evan!"

"Super Evan!" the kids shouted as they ran off happily with their kite.

Evan leaned down to talk to Andy. "If I stay big like this, do you think I really could get a job as a superhero?"

"I don't think it pays very well," Kermit chimed in. "In the comic books, you *never* see those guys getting paid."

They crossed the street and headed toward the playground. Evan glanced at the redbrick school building on the corner. It's so small, he thought.

He suddenly realized that he stood at least two stories tall. If I walk over there, I can see into the second-floor classrooms, he thought.

How will I go to school? Evan wondered. I can't squeeze through the door. I won't fit in Mrs. McGrady's room anymore.

Feeling a wave of sadness roll over him, he turned away from the school building. He heard cheers and shouts. A softball game was underway on the practice diamond.

Evan recognized Billy Denver and Brian Johnson and some of the other kids. He always had to beg to play softball with them. They never wanted

Evan on their team because he wasn't a very good hitter.

He strolled over the grass to the practice diamond. Andy and Kermit ran behind him, struggling to keep up.

Brian was starting to pitch the ball. But he stopped short when he spotted Evan. The ball dropped from his hand and dribbled to the ground.

Players on both teams gasped and shouted.

Evan strode up to Brian on the pitcher's mound. Brian's eyes bulged in fear as Evan drew near. Brian raised his hands to shield himself. "Don't hurt me!" he pleaded.

"Hey — it's Evan!" Billy exclaimed. "Look, guys! It's Evan!"

Kids from both teams gathered around, murmuring excitedly, nervously.

Brian slowly lowered his hands and stared up at the giant Evan. "Wow! It really *is* you! Evan — how did you *do* that?"

"What happened to you?" another kid cried.

"He's been working out!" Andy told them.

The kids laughed. Very tense laughter.

Andy always has a joke for everything, Evan thought.

"Uh . . . want to play?" Brian asked. "You can be on my team."

"No. My team!" Billy insisted.

"No way! He's on my team!" Brian shouted. "We're one man short, remember?"

"Don't say *short* around Evan!" Andy joked.
Everyone laughed again.

Billy and Brian continued to fight over which team would get Evan. Evan stood back and enjoyed the argument. He picked up a wooden bat. It had always seemed so heavy before. Now it felt as light as a pencil.

Billy won the argument. "You can bat now, Evan," he said, grinning up at him.

"How can I pitch to him? He's a giant!" Brian complained.

"Pitch it really high," Evan suggested.

"Evan, do your mom and dad know you grew like this?" Billy asked, walking to home plate beside Evan.

Evan swallowed hard. He hadn't thought about his parents. They'd be getting home from work soon. They weren't going to be happy about this. How would he break the news to them? he wondered.

And then he thought: I won't *have* to break the news to them. They'll see for themselves what has happened!

He stepped up to the plate and swung the bat onto his shoulder. "Wish we had a bigger bat," he muttered. It was a little larger than a drinking straw.

"Get a hit!" Billy shouted from behind the backstop.

"Get a hit, Evan!" several other players called.

Brian's first pitch sailed past Evan's ankles.

"Higher!" Evan called out to him. "You'll have to throw it higher."

"I'm trying!" Brian grumbled. He pulled the softball back and tossed it again.

This time, the pitch flew past Evan's knees.

"It's hard to throw that high," Brian complained. "This isn't fair."

"Strike him out, Brian!" the first baseman cried. "You can do it. Evan always strikes out!"

It's true, Evan thought unhappily. I do usually strike out.

He gripped the little bat tighter, poising it over his shoulder. He suddenly wondered if being so big would make a difference.

Maybe he'd just strike out *bigger*!

Brian's next pitch sailed higher. Evan swung hard. The bat hit the softball with a deafening *thwack* — and cracked in two.

The ball sailed up, up, up. Off the playground. Over the school. And out of sight, somewhere in the next block.

Cheers and cries of amazement rang out over the diamond.

Evan watched the ball fly out of sight. Then he leaped joyfully in the air and began running the bases.

The longest home run in the history of the world!

It took only four steps between bases. He had

just rounded second base when he heard the sirens.

Evan turned his eyes to the street in time to see two fire trucks squeal around the corner. The trucks pulled right up onto the playground grass and came roaring toward the softball diamond, sirens blaring.

Evan stopped at third base.

The sirens cut off as the two fire engines skidded to a halt along the first base line.

Evan's mouth dropped open as Conan Barber leaped out of the first truck. Several black-uniformed firefighters dropped to the ground behind Conan.

"There he is!" Conan cried, pointing furiously at Evan. "That's him! Get him!"

20

Grim-faced firefighters began hoisting heavy fire-hoses off the trucks. Others moved toward Evan, hatchets clutched menacingly in their hands.

"That's him!" Conan shrieked. "He's the one who put me in the tree and wrecked my parents' fence!"

"Huh?" Still standing on third base, Evan froze in shock.

Was this really happening?

The playground rang out with shouts of surprise. But the voices were drowned out by more sirens.

Evan saw flashing red lights. And then two black-and-white police cars roared over the grass, screeching up behind the fire engines.

A man and woman came running behind the police cars. "That's the one!" they called breathlessly, pointing at Evan. "That's the one who crushed the car. We saw him do it!"

The firefighters were busily connecting the

hoses to hydrants at the curb. Blue-uniformed police swarmed on to the field. The kids on the two softball teams huddled together on the pitcher's mound. They all seemed dazed and frightened.

"He tried to kill me!" Conan was shouting to a woman police officer. "That giant put me in a tree and left me there!"

"He crushed a car!" a woman screamed.

Evan hadn't moved from third base. He gazed past the fire engines to Andy and Kermit. They stood near the backstop. Kermit had the dumb, toothy grin on his face.

Andy had her hands cupped around her mouth. She was shouting something to Evan. But he couldn't hear her over the wail of sirens and the excited shouts and cries of everyone in the playground.

Some of the police and fire officers huddled together, talking rapidly. They kept glancing up at Evan as they talked.

What are they going to do to me? Evan wondered, frozen in fear.

Should I run? Should I try to explain?

More people came hurrying across the playground. As soon as they spotted Evan, their expressions turned to surprise and amazement.

They're all staring at me, Evan realized. They're pointing at me as if I'm some kind of freak.

I *am* some kind of freak! he admitted to himself.

Firefighters formed a line, holding their hatchets waist-high. Others readied the firehoses, aiming them up at Evan's chest.

Evan heard more sirens. More police cars rolled on to the playground.

A young police officer with wavy red hair and a red mustache stepped up to Evan. "What — is — your — name?" he shouted, speaking each word slowly, as if maybe Evan didn't speak English.

"Uh . . . Evan. Evan Ross," Evan called down.

"Do you come from another planet?" the officer shouted.

"Huh?" Evan couldn't help himself. He burst out laughing.

He heard some of the softball players laughing, too.

"I live in Atlanta," he shouted down to the officer. "Around the corner. On Brookridge Drive."

Several officers and firefighters held their ears. Evan's voice came out louder than he had planned.

Evan took a step toward them.

The firefighters raised a firehose. Several others readied their hatchets.

"He's dangerous!" Evan heard Conan shout. "Watch out! He's really dangerous!"

That got everyone shouting and screaming.

The playground was filling with people. Neighborhood people. Kids and their parents. Cars stopped and people climbed out to see why the crowd had gathered.

More police cars bumped over the grass. Their wailing sirens added to the deafening noise, the shouts and cries, the frightened murmurs.

The noise. The staring eyes. The pointed fingers.

It all started to make Evan dizzy.

He felt his legs tremble. His forehead throbbed.

The police had formed a line. They started to circle Evan.

As they closed in, Evan felt himself explode. "I can't take any more!" he screamed, raising his fists. "Stop it! Stop it! All of you! Get away! Leave me alone! I mean it!"

Silence as the sirens cut off. The voices hushed.

And then Evan heard the red-haired police officer shout to the others: "He's turned violent. We have to bring him down!"

21

Evan didn't have time to be frightened.

The firehoses chugged and gurgled — then shot out thick streams of water.

Evan ducked low. Dove forward. Tried to get away from the roaring water.

The force of the water stream ripped the ground to his side.

Evan dodged to the other side.

Wow! That's powerful! he thought, horrified. The water is strong enough to knock me over!

Frightened shouts rose up over the roar of the water.

Evan plunged through the line of dark-uniformed police officers — and kept running. "Don't shoot!" he screamed. "Don't shoot me! I'm not from another planet! I'm just a boy!"

He didn't know if they could hear him or not.

He dodged past several startled onlookers. A long hook-and-ladder stood in his path.

He stopped. Glanced back.

Firefighters were turning the hoses. The powerful spray arced high. Water crashed to the ground just behind Evan, loud as thunder.

Kids and parents were running in all directions, frantic, frightened expressions locked on their faces.

Evan took a deep breath. Bent his knees. And leaped over the fire truck in his path.

He heard shouts of surprise behind him. He vaulted high over the truck. Landed hard on the other side. Stumbled. Caught his balance.

Then, ducking low, his arms stretched out in front of him, Evan ran.

His long legs carried him away quickly. As he reached the street, a low tree branch popped up as if from nowhere.

Evan dipped his head just in time.

Leaves scratched over his forehead, but he kept running.

Got to watch out for tree branches, he warned himself. Got to remember that I'm two stories tall.

Breathing hard, he plunged across the street. The late afternoon sun was lowering behind the trees. The shadows were longer now, and darker. Evan's shadow seemed a mile long as it stretched out in front of him.

He heard the rise and fall of shrill sirens behind him. Heard angry shouts. Heard the thud of footsteps, people running after him.

Where can I hide? he asked himself. Where will I be safe?

Home?

No. That's the first place the police will look. Where? Where?

It was so hard to think clearly. They were close behind him, he knew. Chasing him. Eager to bring him down.

If only he could stop somewhere, close his eyes, shut them all out, and think. Then maybe he could come up with a plan.

But he knew he had to keep running.

His head throbbed. His chest ached.

His long legs were taking him quickly away from the playground. But he still felt awkward, with his sneakers so far below him and his head so high in the trees.

I'll hide out at Kermit's house, he thought.

Then he quickly decided that was a bad idea, too.

"I can't get *in* Kermit's house!" he cried out loud. "I'm too big!"

And then he had a truly frightening thought: "I can't fit in *any* house!"

Where will I sleep? he wondered. And then: Will they let me sleep?

Can't the police see I'm just a boy? Evan asked himself bitterly. He turned the corner and ran past his house. The lights were all off. The door closed. No car in the driveway.

His parents hadn't come home from work.

He kept running. Running across yards. Ducking low. Trying to hide behind shrubs and tall hedges.

Can't they see I'm a boy? Not a creature from another planet?

Why do they think I'm so dangerous?

It's all Conan's fault, Evan decided. Conan got the firefighters and police all crazy with his wild stories.

His wild, *true* stories.

And now where can I run? Where can I hide?

The answer came to him as he neared Kermit's house. Two doors down, a lot had been cleared. And an enormous stack of lumber had been piled at the back. Someone was about to build a house on the lot.

Breathing hard, sweat pouring down his broad forehead, Evan turned and ran across the lot. He ducked behind the tall pile of lumber. And stopped.

He dropped to his knees and leaned against the lumber stack, struggling to catch his breath. He wiped the sweat off his forehead with the sleeve of his T-shirt.

Maybe I'll hide here for a while, he thought. He lowered himself to a sitting position.

If I sit down and hunch my shoulders, the lumber pile hides me from the street. And it's shady and cool behind it. And I can keep an eye on Kermit's house from here.

Yes. This is a good hiding spot for now, Evan decided. Then, after dark, I'll sneak over to my house and try to explain to my parents what happened.

He leaned his back against the lumber pile and shut his eyes.

He had just started to relax a little when he heard a voice cry: "Got him!"

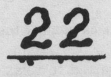

22

Evan's eyes shot open.

He tried to scramble to his feet.

But then he saw who had shouted.

"Kermit!" he cried angrily. "You scared me to death!"

Kermit flashed his annoying grin. "I *knew* you'd hide here, Evan," he said, smirking. "I'm so smart."

Kermit turned and called out, "He's back here! I was right!"

A few seconds later, Andy gingerly poked her head behind the stack of lumber. Her eyes studied Evan for a few seconds. Then a smile crossed her face.

"You're okay?" she asked softly. "I was so worried —"

"Yeah. I'm okay — for now," Evan replied bitterly.

"The whole town is after you!" Kermit exclaimed. "It's really awesome! It's like a movie!"

"I don't *want* to be in a movie!" Evan griped. "This movie is too scary."

"They've got guns and everything!" Kermit continued excitedly, ignoring Evan's complaint. "And did you see those firehoses? It's amazing! They all want to catch you!"

"They think you're an alien from outer space," Andy added, shaking her head.

"And who told them that? Conan?" Evan asked bitterly.

"Conan made them believe you're real dangerous," Kermit said, grinning that grin Evan hated so much.

"I *am* dangerous!" Evan declared. He growled menacingly at Kermit.

The growl shocked the grin off Kermit's face.

Evan turned to Andy. "What am I going to do? I can't run and hide for the rest of my life. They're going to catch me. If you two tracked me down, the police will track me down, too."

Evan let out a long, frightened sigh. "There's nowhere I can hide. I'm too big to hide! So what can I do? What?"

Andy scratched her arm. She knotted up her face, thinking hard. "Well . . ."

And suddenly Evan knew exactly what to do.

Watching Andy, Evan knew how to solve the whole problem.

23

Evan jumped to his feet. His heart began to pound. For the first time in hours, a big smile spread across his face.

"Evan — what's wrong?" Andy demanded. His sudden move had startled her.

"I know what we can do!" Evan declared. "Everything is going to be okay!"

"Get down!" Kermit cried. "I hear sirens. They'll see you."

In his excitement, Evan had forgotten that he was taller than the lumber pile. He dropped back to his knees. Even on his knees, he was a lot taller than Kermit and Andy.

The sirens blared louder. Closer.

Evan gazed around. The sun had fallen behind the trees. The sky was evening gray now. The air grew cooler.

"We've got to hurry," Evan told them. He put a hand on Kermit's slender shoulder. "Kermit, you've got to help me."

Behind his glasses, Kermit's little mouse eyes bulged with excitement. "Me? What can I do?"

"The blue mixture," Evan said, holding on to his cousin's shoulder. "Remember the blue mixture?"

"Wh-which one?" Kermit stammered.

"The one that shrank my mosquito bite!" Andy chimed in. She suddenly realized what Evan was thinking.

"That's right," Evan explained to Kermit. "Watching Andy scratch her arm reminded me. That blue mixture of yours shrank the mosquito bite instantly."

"Maybe it can shrink Evan, too!" Andy exclaimed excitedly.

Kermit nodded, thinking hard. "Yeah. Maybe it can."

"I'll rub it all over my body, and I'll shrink back to my normal size," Evan said happily.

"It'll work! I *know* it will!" Andy cried enthusiastically. She let out a cheer and jumped up and down. Then she tugged Kermit's arm. "Come on, Kermit. Hurry! Let's get to your basement. You still have the blue mixture, don't you?"

Kermit narrowed his eyes, trying to remember. "I think so," he told them. "A lot of stuff got wrecked, remember? But I think I have it."

"He has to have it!" Evan cried. "He *has* to!"

Evan climbed to his feet. "Come on. Hurry."

They heard sirens. Loud and near.

Kermit peered around the lumber pile toward the street. "A police car!" he whispered. "They're cruising this block."

"You'd better wait here," Andy warned Evan.

Evan shook his head. "No way. I'm coming with you. I want to get that blue mixture as fast as I can."

He ducked his head. "We can walk through the backyards. No one will see us."

"But, Evan —" Andy started to protest.

She stopped when Evan stepped away from the lumber pile and started loping quickly across the backyard toward Kermit's house.

Dogface greeted them in the driveway. The sheepdog barked happily, jumping up on Kermit, nearly knocking him to the ground.

"Shhh. Quiet, boy! Quiet!" Kermit cried, petting the dog, trying to stop his barks. "We don't want anyone to hear us."

Dogface gazed up at Evan — and got very quiet. The dog slumped across the driveway. It stared up suspiciously at Evan, panting hard, its stubby tail wagging furiously.

Evan's eyes darted up and down the driveway. No car. "Your mom isn't home yet, Kermit," he said.

"She must be working late," Kermit replied. "That's good news. This is our lucky day!"

Evan let out a bitter laugh. "For sure. Lucky day," he muttered.

Kermit and Andy hurried to the kitchen door. Evan started to follow. Then he remembered he didn't fit in the house.

"Wait right there," Andy instructed him. "Make sure no one sees you."

Evan nodded. "Hurry — please!"

He watched them disappear through the door. Then he sat down behind the house. He motioned for Dogface to come over to him. He felt like holding on to something.

But the big dog just stared back and wouldn't budge.

The whole town is looking for me, Evan thought unhappily. The whole town is looking for a *giant* me. But they'll never find the giant me. Because in a few seconds, I'll shrink back to normal size.

Then everything will be okay again.

He raised his eyes to the house. What is keeping Andy and Kermit? he wondered. Can't they find the bottle of blue liquid?

He took a deep breath. Don't panic, Evan, he instructed himself. They've only been in the house a few seconds. They'll be out soon. And everything will be okay.

To pass the time, he counted slowly to ten. Then he counted slowly to ten again.

He was about to start counting one more time

when the screen door flew open. Kermit stepped out, carrying the blue beaker. Andy followed right behind.

"Found it!" Kermit cried happily.

Evan jumped to his knees. He reached out eagerly. "Quick — let me have it."

Kermit stretched up his hand. Evan grabbed for the glass beaker.

It slipped out of his grasp.

It started to fall.

"Ohhh!" Evan let out a horrified moan — and caught the beaker just before it crashed against the driveway.

"Wow! Nice catch!" Kermit exclaimed.

Evan's heart had leaped to his mouth. He took a deep breath. He grasped the beaker tightly in his hand. "Close one," he murmured. The beaker was so tiny in his hand, like something made for a dollhouse.

They heard sirens in the distance.

The search for the giant Evan was still on.

"I — I hope this mixture works," Evan declared.

He raised the beaker. Tilted it upside down over his other hand. Waited.

And waited.

Finally, a tiny blue drop of liquid dripped on to Evan's palm.

Nothing more.

He shook the beaker. Hard. Harder. The way

he shook a ketchup bottle when the ketchup stuck.

Then he raised the beaker to his eye and peered inside.

A few seconds later, he let out a long, sad sigh. He tossed the bottle disgustedly onto the grass. "It's empty," Evan reported. "Totally empty."

24

"I knew there wasn't much left," Kermit murmured, shaking his head.

The empty bottle rolled under a shrub. Dogface walked over and sniffed it.

"I'm doomed," Evan muttered. Forgetting how strong he was, he angrily kicked a pebble down the driveway. The pebble sailed up into the air and disappeared over the house across the street.

"Be careful," Andy warned. "You could break a window."

"Who cares?" Evan snapped. "My life is ruined."

"No way!" Kermit cried. "You'll be okay, Evan." He started running to the house. "Be right back!"

"Kermit, where are you going?" Evan called glumly.

"To mix up another batch!" Kermit replied. "It will only take me a few seconds, Evan. I've got all the ingredients."

Evan could feel his sadness lifting. "Do you really think you can do it?" he asked his cousin.

"No problem," Kermit replied, flashing Evan a thumbs-up sign. "I think I remember what I put in it. I'll mix up more blue shrinking stuff and be back in a jiffy."

Kermit disappeared into the house. "I'm coming, too!" Andy called after him. She turned back to Evan. "I can try to clean up some of the lab while Kermit mixes the liquid. If Kermit's mom gets home and sees the basement, you'll be in big trouble."

Evan let out a weak laugh. *"Big* trouble. Very funny, Annnndrea. You're a riot."

"Don't call me Andrea," she shot back, ignoring his sarcasm. He watched her hurry into the house.

Dogface got tired of sniffing the blue bottle. The sheepdog lumbered across the yard to inspect the fence that Evan had knocked down earlier.

Evan sighed. I wonder if my own dog will recognize me now? he thought. Trigger, Evan's cocker spaniel, had been the first to eat Monster Blood. The dog had grown bigger than a horse.

I wonder if Trigger ever has nightmares about that? Evan asked himself.

He knew he'd be having nightmares about today for a long time to come.

He glanced at his watch. Almost dinnertime. His parents would be getting home soon. And

Kermit's mom would be pulling up the driveway at any minute.

"Wow. She'll be surprised when she sees *me!*" Evan exclaimed out loud.

He turned to the house in time to see Kermit step out. He was carrying a fresh bottle of blue liquid. "See? No problem!" Kermit declared.

Evan carefully took the bottle from Kermit's hand.

Andy walked over, her eyes raised to Evan's. "Go ahead. Rub it all over," she urged. "Hurry!"

Evan carefully poured a puddle of blue liquid into his palm. Then he rubbed it onto his cheeks, his forehead, his neck.

He poured more into his hand. He rubbed blue liquid onto his arms. Then he raised his T-shirt and rubbed some on his chest.

Please let it work, he prayed silently. Please let it work.

He turned to Andy and Kermit. "See any change?"

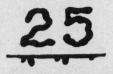

25

Andy's mouth dropped open.

Kermit's eyes bulged, and he uttered a choking sound.

"Well?" Evan demanded eagerly. "Do you see any change? Do you?"

"Uh . . . well . . . uh . . ." Kermit sputtered.

"You turned blue!" Andy cried.

"Excuse me?" Evan demanded. He knew he hadn't heard her correctly.

"Your skin — it's bright blue!" Andy wailed, pressing her hands against her cheeks.

"My — what?" Evan shrieked. "You mean — HIC! —" A powerful hiccup made his entire body shake.

Evan stared down at his hands.

"They — they're blue!" he cried. "HIC!"

Another hiccup burst from his open mouth. His enormous body shook as if struck by an earthquake.

Frantically, he pulled up the T-shirt and stared at his stomach. His blue stomach.

His arms. His chest. All blue. Bright blue.

"HIC!"

"I don't believe it!" Evan screamed. "I'm bright blue, and — HIC! — I've got the hiccups!"

He glared down furiously at Kermit.

Kermit was so frightened, his legs trembled and his knees actually knocked together. "I — I can fix it," he called up to Evan. "N-no problem! I just mixed it up wrong. I'll be right back with another mixture."

He ran to the house. At the screen door, he turned back to Evan. "Don't go anywhere — okay?"

Evan let out a furious roar, interrupted by a deafening hiccup. *"Where can I go?"* he shrieked at the top of his lungs. *"Where can I — HIC! — go?!"*

The door slammed behind Kermit.

Evan let out another roar, clenching his blue fists and shaking his blue arms over his head. He paced back and forth on the driveway, hiccupping every few seconds.

"Try to calm down a little," Andy called up to him. "People will hear you."

"I — I — HIC! — can't calm down!" Evan complained bitterly. "Look at me!"

"But the neighbors will hear you. Or see you," Andy warned. "They'll call the police."

Evan replied with a hiccup that nearly knocked him off his feet.

Kermit came running out of the house. He raised another bottle of blue liquid to Evan. "Here! Try this!"

"HIC!" Evan declared. He grasped the bottle in his blue hand.

Without saying another word, he turned the bottle upside down. With quick, frantic motions, he splashed the blue liquid all over him. Over his cheeks. His forehead. His hands and arms. His chest.

He rolled up his jeans and rubbed the mixture onto his knees and legs. He pulled off his socks and sneakers and smoothed the blue liquid over his ankles and feet.

"It's *got* to work!" he cried. "This time, it's *got* to!"

Andy and Kermit stared up at him eagerly.

They waited.

Evan waited.

Nothing happened. No change at all.

Then Evan began to feel it.

"Hey — I'm tingling!" he announced happily.

He felt the same electric tingling he had felt before. The itchy feeling he had every time he was about to grow a little more.

"Yes!" Evan cheered. "Yes!"

The tingling grew sharper, stronger, as it spread over his entire body.

"It's working! I can — HIC! — feel it!" Evan shouted. "It's really working! I'm tingling! I'm itching! I can feel it! It's working!"

"No, it isn't," Andy murmured quietly.

26

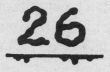

"Huh?" Evan narrowed his eyes at her.

The tingling became a violent itch. He started to scratch. But pulled back his hand because his skin felt so strange.

"It . . . didn't . . . work. . . ." Andy said sadly, her voice trembling.

"Yuck! He looks so gross!" Kermit declared, making a disgusted face.

"Huh? HIC!" Evan replied.

He uttered a horrified gasp as he stared at his arms. "F-f-feathers!" he stammered in a high, shrill voice.

He checked out his arms. His stomach. His legs.

"Noooooo!" A long, low wail burst from his chest.

His entire body was covered in fluffy white feathers.

"Noooo — HIC! — ooooooooo!"

"I'm sorry," Kermit said, shaking his head. "I

don't know what I'm doing wrong. I thought I had the mixture right this time."

"You look like a big eagle," Andy commented. "Except eagles aren't blue."

"HIC!" Evan cried.

"And eagles don't get hiccups," Andy added. She gazed up at him with concern. "Poor Evan. That must itch like crazy. You're having a real bad day."

Evan frantically scratched his feathery chest. "It can't get any worse than this," he muttered.

And then he saw a police car pull up in front of the house.

27

"HIC!" Evan cried. He backed off the driveway and crouched low against the back wall of the house. "The police!" he whispered.

His throat tightened in panic. His feathers all stood up on end.

What should I do? he asked himself, pressed against the house, ducking his head. Should I run? Should I give myself up?

"One more try!" Kermit cried, leaping into the house. "Let me try one more mixture. I think I can get it this time!"

The door slammed behind him.

"Hurry!" Andy called from the driveway. "The police — they're climbing out of their car."

"How many are there?" Evan whispered. His feathers itched, but he was too frightened to scratch.

"Two," Andy replied, staring through the gray evening light to the street. "They look kind of mean."

A sudden cool gust of wind ruffled Evan's feathers. His huge body trembled.

"They're walking up the driveway," Andy reported. "They're going to be here in a few seconds!"

"I'd better make a run for it," Evan declared. He took one step away from the house and nearly fell. It was hard to run when your feet were covered with stiff, prickly feathers.

His entire body itched. He pressed himself against the house again. "I'm doomed," he murmured to himself.

"They stopped to check out the front door," Andy told him. "You've still got a few seconds."

"Hurry, Kermit! Hurry!" Evan urged out loud.

He turned to the kitchen door. No sign of Kermit.

Would Kermit get the mixture right this time? Could he get the mixture to Evan before the two police officers entered the backyard?

The screen door opened. Kermit burst out. He tripped on the back stoop. The blue bottle nearly went flying.

He caught his balance. He handed the bottle up to Evan. "Good luck!" Kermit called up to Evan. Kermit raised both hands. He had his fingers tightly crossed on both hands.

"Here come the police," Andy warned. "They're walking really fast now."

The bottle trembled in Evan's hand. He turned

it upside down. It puddled in his enormous, feathery palm.

Frantically, he began rubbing it over his feathers, over his blue skin. Splashing it wildly. Pouring it over his body.

Please work! he silently urged it. Please work!

He waited.

Kermit stared up at him hopefully, his fingers still crossed.

"They're here!" Andy reported from the driveway.

Evan gulped.

The mixture hadn't worked.

He hadn't changed. Not a bit.

The two dark-uniformed officers approached the back of the house. "Hello, there," one of them called to Andy.

28

Evan heard a loud POP.

He uttered a startled cry as he felt himself falling. Falling to the ground.

He reached out a hand and steadied himself against the house.

It took him a second or two to realize that he hadn't fallen. He had shrunk.

The two officers stepped into the backyard. One was very tall. The other was short and plump. "Sorry to bother you kids," the tall one said. "But we got a call from a neighbor."

"A call? About what?" Andy demanded. She cast a surprised glance at Evan. She didn't expect to see him back to normal.

"Did you kids see a giant in the neighborhood?" the short officer asked. He narrowed his eyes at them, trying to appear tough.

"A giant? What kind of giant?" Kermit asked innocently.

"A giant kid," the short officer replied.

Evan, Andy, and Kermit shook their heads. "He didn't come back here," Andy told them.

"No. We didn't see him," Evan said. He couldn't keep a smile from crossing his face. His voice was back to normal, too.

The tall officer pushed his cap back on his head. "Well, if you see him, be careful," he warned. "He's dangerous."

"He's very dangerous," the short officer added. "Call us right away — okay?"

"Okay," all three kids replied in unison.

The officers gave the backyard one last look. Then they turned and headed back down the driveway to their car.

As soon as they were gone, Evan burst into a long, happy cheer. Andy and Kermit joined in, clapping him joyfully on the back, slapping high fives all around.

"Am I a genius or what?" Kermit demanded, grinning his toothy grin.

"Or what!" Evan joked.

They were still laughing and celebrating Evan's return to Evan-size when Kermit's mom pulled up the driveway. As she climbed out of her car, she appeared surprised to find them outdoors.

"Sorry I'm so late," she called. She hugged Kermit. "How was your afternoon?"

Kermit glanced at Evan. Then he smiled at

his mother. "Oh, it was kind of boring," he told her.

"Yeah. Kind of boring," Andy repeated.

"Kind of boring," Evan agreed.

Evan knew he'd have nightmares about what had happened to him. And that night, he had a really scary one. In the dream, he was a giant boy being chased by giant rats. The rats all looked like Kermit.

Evan sat up in the dark, shivering all over.

"Just a nightmare," he murmured, glancing at his clock radio. Midnight. "It was just a nightmare."

He sat up straight, wiping sweat off his forehead with his pajama-top sleeve. I need a glass of cold water, he decided.

He started to climb out of bed — but stopped when he saw what a steep drop it was to the floor.

Huh? What's going on? he asked himself.

He tried to click on the bedtable lamp. But it towered high above him, way beyond his reach.

He stood up on the bed. As his eyes adjusted to the dim light, he saw that his bed seemed to stretch on forever. A lump in the bedspread curled up over Evan's head.

I — I'm short! he realized. I'm as short as a mouse!

Kermit!

Kermit strikes again! Evan thought bitterly.

He made the blue shrinking mixture too powerful.

I shrank — and shrank — and shrank. And now I'm as tiny as a mouse.

"I'll pound Kermit! I really will!" Evan cried. His voice came out as tiny mouse squeaks.

Standing on the edge of his bed, staring down, down — miles down — to the floor, Evan heard a rumbling sound. Loud panting that sounded like a strong wind through the trees.

A big head popped up in front of him. Two dark eyes.

"No! Trigger! Go back to sleep!" Evan pleaded in his little mouse voice. "No! Trigger — down!"

Evan's squeaks had awakened the cocker spaniel.

Evan felt the dog's hot breath blow across his face.

"Yuck! Dog breath!" he squeaked.

Then he felt sharp teeth close around his waist. Felt himself tilted sideways. Felt the hot, wet saliva of Trigger's mouth as the dog secured Evan between its teeth.

"Trigger — down! Put me down!" Evan begged.

He was bounced hard now. The dog teeth tightened their grip.

"Trigger! Put me down! Where are you taking me?"

Through the dark hallway. The hot breath blowing over Evan's helpless body.

Into his parents' room. Evan gazed up to see his mom and dad getting ready for bed.

Mr. Ross leaned over the dog. "What have you got there, Trigger? Did you find a bone?"

"Uh . . . Dad? Dad?" Evan squeaked up at him. "Dad? It's me? Do you see me? Dad? Uh . . . I think we have a little problem!"

Add *more*

Goosebumps

to your collection . . .
A chilling preview of
what's next from
R.L. STINE

IT CAME FROM
BENEATH
THE SINK!

1

Before my brother and I found the strange little creature under the sink, we were a normal happy family. In fact, I'd have to say we were very lucky.

But our luck quickly changed when we pulled the creature from its dark hiding place.

The sad, frightening story begins on the day we moved.

"Here we are, kids." Dad honked the horn happily as we rounded the corner onto Maple Lane and pulled up in front of our new house. "Ready for the big move, Kitty Kat?"

My dad is the only one who can get away with calling me Kitty Kat. My real name is Katrina (ugh!) Merton, but only the teachers call me Katrina. To everyone else I'm simply Kat.

"Definitely, Dad!" I shouted. I jumped out of the station wagon.

"Rowf! Rowf!" Killer, our cocker spaniel, barked in agreement and followed me out onto the sidewalk.

Daniel, my goofy little brother, is the one who named the dog. What a dumb name. Killer is afraid of *everything*. The only thing he kills is his rubber ball!

Daniel and I had biked past the new house plenty of times already. It's only three blocks away from where we used to live, on East Main.

But I still couldn't believe we'd be *living* here. I mean, I always thought our old house was pretty great. But this place is awesome!

Three stories high, sitting up on its own little hill, with butter-yellow shutters and at least a dozen windows. A wide porch wraps around the whole house. The front yard must be about the size of a football field.

It's not a house — it's a mansion!

Well, *practically* a mansion. Enormous — but not exactly fancy. What Mom calls "a comfortable old shoe kind of house."

Actually, today it really looked messy and old. A few of the shutters hung crookedly, the grass needed mowing, and the whole place seemed to be covered with an inch of dust.

But as Mom said, "Nothing that can't be taken care of with a good cleaning, a coat of paint, and a few bangs with the hammer."

Mom, Dad, and Daniel climbed out of the car, and we all stood staring excitedly at the house. Today, I'd finally get to see the inside!

Mom pointed to the second floor. "See that big

balcony?" she asked. "That's the room where your father and I will sleep. The next room over is Daniel's."

She gave my hand a little squeeze. "The little balcony — that's outside *your* room, Kat." She beamed.

My very own private porch! I leaned over and gave Mom a big hug. "I love it already," I whispered into her ear.

Naturally, Daniel started whining immediately. He's ten years old, but most of the time he acts as if he's about two.

"How come Kat's room has a balcony — and mine doesn't?" he complained. "It's not fair! I want a balcony, too!"

"Get a life, Daniel," I muttered. "Mom, tell him to be quiet. Don't I get *something* for being two years older?"

Well, almost two years older. My birthday was in four days.

"Quiet, kids," Mom ordered. "Daniel, you don't have a balcony. But you are getting something neat, too — bunk beds. So Carlo can sleep over whenever you want."

"Excellent!" Daniel shouted. Carlo is Daniel's best friend. They're always together — and always bugging me.

Daniel is okay — most of the time. But he insists on being right. Dad calls him Mr. Know-It-All.

And sometimes Dad calls Daniel the Human Tornado, because he runs around like a whirlwind and makes unbelievable messes.

I'm a lot more like my Dad — sort of calm and quiet. Well, usually calm. And we both have the same favorite foods — lasagna, really sour garlic pickles, and mocha-chip ice cream.

I even look like my father, tall and thin with a lot of freckles and reddish hair. I usually wear my hair in a ponytail. Dad doesn't have much hair to worry about.

Daniel looks more like my mother. Straight, light brown hair that's always falling in his eyes, and what Mom calls a "sturdy" build. (That means he's chunky.)

Today, Daniel was definitely in Human Tornado mode. He ran up onto the big green lawn and began spinning around in a circle. "It's huge," he shouted. "It's gigantic. It's . . . it's . . . it's super-house!"

He collapsed in a heap on the grass. "And this is the super-yard! Hey, Kat, look at me — I'm Super-Daniel!"

"You're super-dumb," I told him, messing up his hair with both hands.

"Hey, quit it!" Daniel yelped. He pulled out his super-soaker gun and squirted the front of my T-shirt. "You're captured," he announced. "You are my prisoner!"

"I don't think so," I replied, tugging on the water pistol. "Give up the gun!" I commanded. I pulled harder. "Let go!"

"Okay!" Daniel grinned. He loosened his grip so suddenly that I staggered backwards — and fell on to the sidewalk.

"What a klutz!" Daniel snickered.

I knew how to get him. I zoomed up the porch steps. "Hey, Daniel," I called, "I'm going to be first in the new house!"

"No way!" he exclaimed, scrambling up off the lawn. He hurled himself at the steps and grabbed me by the ankle. "Me first! Me first!"

That's when Dad walked up the driveway, carrying an overstuffed cardboard box with KITCHEN written on the side. Two moving men followed, hauling our big blue couch.

"Hey, stop goofing around! Mom and I really need your help today. That's why we allowed you to miss a school day," he called. "Daniel, walk Killer — and make sure he has food and water. Kat, keep an eye on Daniel.

"And Kat, clean the inside of the kitchen cabinets, okay?" Dad added. "Mom wants to start putting the dishes and pots away."

"Sure, Dad," I answered. I saw Daniel rummaging through a box on the lawn. The box was marked CARDS AND COMICS.

"Hey, where's the dog?" I yelled to him.

He shrugged.

"Daniel!" I frowned. "I don't see Killer anywhere. Where is he?"

He dropped a stack of baseball cards. "Okay, okay, I'll go find him," he mumbled. He stood up and made his way to the driveway, calling the dog's name.

As soon as he disappeared around the side of the house, I hurried to the box marked CARDS AND COMICS and checked through it. Sure enough, the little brat had stolen some of my comics.

I tucked them under my arm and walked inside to the kitchen to clean out the cabinets. One quick glance made me groan.

Cabinets filled just about every square inch of the big bright room! Sighing, I yanked paper towels and a bottle of cleaner out of the CLEANING SUPPLIES box and started scrubbing.

Spritz, rub, spritz, rub.

This could take hours!

After I finished a cabinet, I stepped back to admire my work. Then I knelt down in front of the cabinet under the sink.

But something — a squeaky noise, like the sound of a footstep on an old wooden stair — made me stop short.

What is that? I wondered, my heart beating faster.

I slowly opened the cabinet. Tried to peek inside.

I opened it a little wider. A little wider.
I heard the noise again.
My heart was pounding now.
I opened the cabinet door another inch.
And then it grabbed me.
A dark, hairy claw.
It wouldn't let go.
I screamed.

About the Author

R.L. STINE is the author of over three dozen best-selling thrillers and mysteries for young people. Recent titles for teenagers include *I Saw You That Night!*, *Call Waiting*, *Halloween Night II*, *The Dead Girlfriend*, and *The Baby-sitter III*, all published by Scholastic. He is also the author of the *Fear Street* series.

Bob lives in New York City with his wife, Jane, and fourteen-year-old son, Matt.

Get Goosebumps
by R.L. Stine